FIANCÉE
FOR ONE NIGHT

FIANCÉE
FOR ONE NIGHT

BY

TRISH MOREY

MILLS
BOON®

First published in Great Britain 2011
by Mills & Boon, an imprint of Harlequin (UK) Limited.
Large Print edition 2011
Harlequin (UK) Limited, Eton House,
18-24 Paradise Road, Richmond, Surrey TW9 1SR

© Trish Morey 2011

ISBN: 978 0 263 22251 7

Harlequin (UK) policy is to use papers that are natural,
renewable and recyclable products and made from
wood grown in sustainable forests. The logging and
manufacturing process conform to the legal environmental
regulations of the country of origin.

Printed and bound in Great Britain
by CPI Antony Rowe, Chippenham, Wiltshire

This book is dedicated to you, the reader,
the person this book was written for.

Please enjoy FIANCÉE FOR ONE NIGHT.
Much love, as always,

Trish x

CHAPTER ONE

LEO ZAMOS loved it when a plan came together.

Not that he couldn't find pleasure in other, more everyday pursuits. He was more than partial to having a naked woman in his bed, and the more naked the woman the more partial he was inclined to be, and he lived for the blood-dizzying rush from successfully navigating his Maserati Granturismo S at speed around the sixty hairpin turns of the Passa dello Stelvio whenever he was in Italy and got the chance.

Still, nothing could beat the sheer unmitigated buzz that came from conceiving a plan so audacious it could never happen, and then steering it through the ensuing battles, corporate manoeuvrings and around the endless bureaucratic roadblocks to its ultimate conclusion—*and his inevitable success.*

And right now he was on the cusp of his most audacious success yet.

All he needed was a wife.

He stepped from his private jet into the mild Melbourne spring air, refusing to let that one niggling detail ruin his good mood. He was too close to pulling off his greatest coup yet to allow that to happen. He sucked in a lungful of the Avgas-flavoured air and tasted only success as he headed down the stairs to the waiting car. The Culshaw Diamond Corporation, owner and producer of the world's finest pink diamonds and a major powerhouse on the diamond market, had been in the hands of the one big Australian diamond dynasty for ever. Leo had been the one to sense a change in the dynamic of those heading up the business, to detect the hairline cracks that had been starting to show in the Culshaw brothers' management team, though not even he had seen the ensuing scandal coming, the circumstances of which had made the brothers' positions on the board untenable.

There'd been a flurry of interest from all quarters then, but Leo had been the one in pole position. Already he'd introduced Richard Alvarez, head of the team interested in buying the business, to Eric Culshaw senior, an intensely private man who had been appalled by the scandal and just wanted to fade quietly into obscurity. And so now for the first time in its long and previously unsullied history, the Culshaw Diamond Corporation was about to change hands, courtesy of Leo Zamos, broker to billionaires.

Given the circumstances, perhaps he should have seen this latest complication coming. But if Eric Culshaw, married nearly fifty years to his childhood sweetheart, had decreed that he would only do business with people of impeccable family credentials and values, and with Alvarez agreeing to bring his wife along, clearly Leo would just have to find himself a wife too.

Kind of ironic really, given he'd avoided the institution with considerable success all these years. Women did not make the mistake of thinking there was any degree of permanence in the arrangement when they chanced to grace his arm or bed.

Not for long anyway.

But a one-night wife? That much he could handle. The fact he had to have one by eight p.m. tonight was no real problem.

Evelyn would soon find him someone suitable.

After all, it wasn't like he actually needed to get married. A fiancée would do just fine, a fiancée found after no doubt long years of searching for that 'perfect' soulmate—Eric Culshaw could hardly hold the fact they hadn't as yet tied the knot against him, surely?

He had his phone in hand as he nodded to the waiting driver before curling himself into the sleek limousine, thankful they'd cleared customs when they'd landed earlier in Darwin to refuel, and already devising a mental list of the woman's necessary attributes.

Clearly he didn't want just any woman. This one had to be classy, intelligent and charming. The ability to hold a conversation desirable though not essential. It wouldn't necessarily matter if she couldn't, so long as she was easy on the eye.

Evelyn would no doubt be flicking through her contacts, turning up a suitable candidate, before she hung up the phone. Leo allowed himself a flicker of a smile and listened to the burr of a telephone ringing somewhere across the city as his driver pulled effortlessly into the endless stream of airport traffic.

Dispensing with his office two years ago had been one of the best decisions he had ever made. Now, instead of an office, he had a jet that could fly him anywhere in the world, a garage in Italy to house his Maserati, lawyers and financiers on retainer, and a 'virtual' PA who handled everything else he needed with earth-shattering efficiency.

The woman was a marvel. He could only applaud whatever mid-life crisis had prompted her move from employment in a bricks and mortar office to the virtual world. Not that he knew her age, come to think of it. He didn't know any of that personal stuff, he didn't have to, which was half the appeal. No more excuses why someone was late to work, no more hinting about upcoming birthdays or favourite perfumes or sultry looks of availability. He had to endure none of that because he had Evelyn at the end of an email, and given the references she'd proffered and the qualifications and experience she'd quoted in her CV, she'd have to be in her mid-forties at least. No wonder she was over life in the fast lane. Working this way, she'd be able to take a nanna nap whenever she needed it.

The call went to the answering-machine and a toffee butler voice invited him to leave a message, bringing a halt to his self-congratulations. He frowned, not used to wondering where his PA might be. Normally he'd email Evelyn from wherever he happened to be and not have to worry about international connections or time differences. The arrangement worked well, so well in fact that half the time he'd find her answering by return email almost immediately, even when he was sure it must be the middle of the night in Australia. But here in her city at barely eleven in the morning, when she'd known his flight times, he'd simply expected she'd be there to take his call.

'It's Leo,' he growled, after the phone had beeped for him to leave his message. Still he waited, and kept waiting, to see if that announcement would make his virtual PA suddenly pick up. When it was clear no one would, he sighed, rubbed his forehead with his other hand and spat out his message. 'Listen, I need you to find me a woman for tonight…'

'Thank you for your call.'

Leo swore under his breath as the butler terminated the message. Come to think of it, there was a damn good reason he usually emailed.

Eve Carmichael dropped the third peg in as many pairs of leggings and growled in frustration as she reached down to scoop up the offending article and fix the final item on the line. She'd been on tenterhooks all day. *All week more like it.* Ever since she'd known *he* was coming to Melbourne.

She looked up at the weak sun, willing it to dry her washing before Melbourne's notoriously fickle weather suddenly changed seasons on her, and shivered, a spidery shiver that descended down her spine and had nothing to do with the weather and everything to do with the fact Leo Zamos was coming.

And then she glanced down at her watch and the spider ran all the way up again.

Wrong. Leo Zamos was *here*.

It made no difference reminding herself that it was illogical to feel this way. She had no reason, no reason at all, to feel apprehensive. It wasn't like he'd asked her to meet his plane. In fact, it wasn't like he'd made any arrangements to see her at all. Logically, there was no reason why he should—she was his virtual PA after all. He paid her to run around on his behalf via the wonders of the world wide web, not to wait on him hand and foot.

Besides, there was simply no time to shoehorn her into his busy schedule even if he did have reason. She knew that for a fact because she'd emailed him the latest version this morning at six, just before she'd got into the shower and worked out her hot water service had chosen today of all days to die, not twenty-four hours after her clothes line had turned up its toes. A sign? She sure hoped not. If it was, it wasn't a good one.

No wonder she was edgy.

And no wonder this strange sense of foreboding simmered away inside her like a pot of soup that had been on the boil so long that it had thickened and reduced until you could just about stand a spoon in it.

Damn.

She shot a warning look at a cloud threatening to block out the sun and gave the old rotary clothes hoist a spin, hoping to encourage a breeze while cursing the fact that right now she probably had more hope of controlling the weather than she did reining in her own illogical thoughts, and there was no chance of controlling Melbourne's changeable weather.

And then she stiffened her jittery spine and headed back to the house, trying to shake off this irrational urge to do a Rip Van Evelyn and go to sleep until Leo Zamos was safely and surely out of her city.

What the hell was her problem?

Simple, the answer came right back at her, catching her so unawares she forgot to open the back door and almost crashed into it instead.

You're afraid of him.

It stopped her for a moment. Stilled her muscles and cemented her bones with the certainty of someone who had good reason to fear.

Ridiculous, she chided, her mind swiftly writing off the possibility, her breath coming short as she finally forced her fingers to work enough to turn the door handle and let herself in. Leo Zamos was nothing to her but the best hourly rate she'd ever been paid. He was a meal ticket, the ticket to renovating her late-nineteenth-century bungalow she affectionately referred to as the hovel, a ticket to something better in her life and getting it a hell of a lot sooner than it would ever happen otherwise. She just wished she didn't have to spend her renovation money on appliances now, before she even had an idea of what she'd need when the final plans came in.

She glanced upward at the strips of paint shredding from the walls of the laundry and the ivy that was creeping inside through the cracks where sixty years ago her grandfather had tacked it onto the back of the bungalow, and told herself she should be grateful for Leo's business, not a jittery bundle of nerves just because he was in town. Their arrangement worked well. That was all that mattered. That's what she had to concentrate on. Not some long-ago dusty memory that she'd managed to blow out of all proportion.

After all, Leo Zamos certainly wasn't wasting any time fretting about her. And in less than forty-eight hours he'd be gone. There was absolutely nothing at all to be afraid of.

And then she pulled open the creaking laundry door and heard a deep rich voice she recognised instantly, if only because it instinctively made her toes curl and her skin sizzle, *"...find me a woman for tonight..."* and the composure she'd been battling to talk herself into shattered into a million pieces.

She stood there, rooted to the spot, staring at the phone as the call terminated, emotions warring for supremacy inside her. Fury. Outrage. Disbelief. All of them tangled in the barbed wire of something that pricked at her skin and deeper, something she couldn't quite—*or didn't want to*—put a name to.

She ignored the niggling prickle. Homed straight in on the fury.

Who the hell did Leo Zamos think he was?

And what did he think she was? Some kind of pimp?

She swooped around the tiny kitchen, gathering dishes and piling them clattering into the sink. Oh, she knew he had his women. She'd arranged enough Tiffany trinkets and bottles of perfume to be sent to his countless Kristinas and Sabrinas and Audrinas over the last two years—and all with the same terminal message—

Thanks for your company.
Take care.
Leo

—to know he'd barely survive a night without a bed-warmer. But just because he was in her home town it didn't mean he could expect her to find him one.

Pipes groaned and hammered as she spun the hot water tap on fruitlessly, until she realised she needed to boil the kettle first to have any hope of hot water. But finally the sink was filled with suds and the tiny room was full of steam. She shoved her hands into rubber gloves and set upon attacking the stack of dishes and plastic cups, all but hidden under the froth and bubbles.

It had been lucky the machine had cut him off when it had or she might have been forced to pick up the receiver and tell him exactly what he could do with his demands—and that would be one sure way to terminate an income flow she had no way of replacing any time soon.

But, then, did she really want to work with a man who seemed to think it was perfectly acceptable asking his PA to organise him a night-time plaything? Maybe she should just call him herself. Remind him of the duties she had agreed to undertake.

Except that would require talking to him…

Oh, for heavens sake! On impulse she swiped at a tea towel and dried her gloves as she crossed the small living area towards the answering-machine, jabbing at a button before she could change her mind, her brain busy being rational. She dealt with his correspondence all the time, even if mostly by email. Surely she wasn't about to go weak at the knees at the sound of his voice?

And then the message replayed and she heard

the weight of expectation in his pause as he waited for her to pick up—expected her to pick up—before his message. *"Listen, I need you to find me a woman for tonight..."*

And this time her outrage was submerged in a tremor that started in a bloom of heat that radiated across her chest and down her belly, tingling as it shot down her arms and legs. Damn. She shook her hands as if to rid herself of the unwelcome sensations, and headed back to finish the dishes.

So nothing had changed. Because his voice had had the same unsettling effect on her from the very first time she'd heard him speak more than three years ago in a glass-walled boardroom fifty floors above Sydney's CBD. She recalled the way he'd swept out of the lift that day, the air shifting in currents around him in a way that had turned heads and caused more than one woman to stumble as she'd craned her head instead of looking where she was going.

He'd seemed oblivious to his impact, sweeping into the boardroom like he owned it, spicing the air with a mix of musk and wood and citrus and radiating absolute confidence in himself and his role. And no wonder. For whether by sheer force of his personality or acute business acumen, or maybe the dark chocolate over gravel voice that had soothed everyone into submission, he'd successfully brought that deal to a conclusion that day, bringing together an over-eager buyer and a still unconvinced seller, and had had them both smiling as if they'd each got the better part of the deal.

She'd sat in the far corner of the room, taking minutes for her lawyer boss, while another part of her had been busy taking inventory of the man himself even as his rich voice had rippled through her and given birth to all kinds of wayward thoughts she had no business thinking.

Was there anything the man lacked?

Softness, she'd decided, drinking in the details, the thick black hair, the dark-as-night eyes, the strong angles of jaw and nose and the shadowed planes and recesses of his face. No, there was nothing soft about his looks, nothing at all. Even the lips that gave shape to that smooth-as-sin voice were fiercely masculine, a strong mouth she'd imagined as capable of both a smile as a cruel twist.

And then she'd looked up from her notebook to see him staring at her, his eyes narrowing, assessing as, without a move in his head, their focus moved down, and she'd felt his gaze like the touch of his long-fingered hand down her face and throat until with burning cheeks she'd wrenched her eyes away before she felt them wander still lower.

The rest of the meeting had passed in a blur and all she remembered was that every time she had looked up, it had seemed as though he was there, waiting to capture her eyes in his simmering gaze. And all the while the discussions had gone on around her, the finer points of the agreement hammered out, and all she'd been able to think about was discovering the sinful pleasures promised in his deep, dark eyes.

And when she'd gone to help organise coffee and had met him on the way back, she'd felt warmth bloom in her chest and pool in her belly when he'd smiled at her, and let him draw her gently aside with no more than a touch of

his hand to her elbow that had almost had her
bones melt.

'I want you,' he'd whispered, shocking her with
his savage honesty, thrilling her with his message. 'Spend the night with me,' he'd invited, and
his words had poured into all the places that had
been empty and longing all her life, even the tiny
crevices and recesses she'd never known existed
until then.

And she, who had never been noticed in her life
by anyone with such intensity, let alone a powerhouse of masculine perfection like this man, had
done the only possible thing she could do. She'd
said yes, maybe a little too breathlessly, a little
too easily, for he'd growled and pulled her into
a room stacked high with row upon row of files,
already pulling her into his kiss, one hand at her
breast, another curving around her behind even
as he manoeuvred her to the furthest corner of
the room.

Blown away by the man, blown away by the
red-hot magma of sensations surging up inside
her, she hadn't made a move to stop him, hadn't
entertained the possibility until, with one hand

under her shirt and his hard thighs wedged between hers, the door had opened and they'd both stilled and waited while whoever it was searched a row of files, pulling one out with a swish and exiting the room. And he'd pulled her shirt down and pushed the hair back from her face from where he'd loosened it from the coil behind her and asked her name, before he'd kissed her one more time. 'Tonight, Eve,' he'd said, before he'd straightened his tie and gone.

Cups clunked together under the suds and banged into the sides of the tiny sink, a sound reassuringly concrete right now. For this was her reality—a ramshackle bungalow it would cost a fortune to tear down and rebuild and probably more if she decided to renovate and try to preserve what original features might be worth saving.

She finished up the dishes and pulled the plug, letting the water go. She had commitments now. Obligations. A glimpse at her watch told her that her most important obligation would be waking up any minute now.

Would her life be any different if she had spent

the night with Leo that night, if he hadn't been called away with barely a hurried goodbye to sort out a hiccup in the next billionaire deal he had been brokering somewhere halfway around the world, and if they'd actually finished what they'd started in that filing room?

Or given how she'd been incapable of saying no to him that day, maybe her child might simply have been born with skin even more olive, hair a little thicker?

Not that Leo would make those kind of mistakes, she was sure.

No, it was better that nothing had happened that night. He wouldn't be her client now if it had.

Besides, she knew what happened to the women Leo bedded. She could live without one of those terse thank-you notes, even if it did come attached to some pretty piece of bling.

The room darkened and she looked out the window in time to see the first fat drops fall from the dark clouds scudding across the sky and splatter against the glass.

'I thought I warned you,' she growled at the

sky, already making for the back door and forgetting all about Leo Zamos for one short moment.

Until the phone rang again.

CHAPTER TWO

SHE stood there, one hand on the door handle, one thought to the pattering rain growing louder on the tin lean-to roof, and yet Eve made no move towards the clothesline as the phone rang the requisite number of times before the machine cut in, inviting the caller to leave a message.

'Evelyn, it's Leo.'

Redundant really. The flush of heat under her skin told her who it was, and she was forced to admit that even when he sounded half-annoyed, he still had the most amazing voice. She could almost feel the stroke of it across her heated skin, almost feel it cup her elbow, as his hand once had.

'I've sent you an email,' Leo continued, 'or half of one, but this is urgent and I really need to speak with you. If you're home, can you pick up?'

Annoyance slid down her spine. Of course it

was urgent. Or it no doubt seemed urgent to Leo Zamos. A night without a woman to entertain him? It was probably unthinkable. It was also hardly her concern. And still the barbed wire prickling her skin and her psyche tangled tighter around her, squeezing her lungs, and she wished he'd just hang up so she could breathe again.

'Damn it, Evelyn!' he growled, his voice a velvet glove over an iron fist that would wake up the dead, let alone Sam if he kept this up. 'It's eleven a.m. on a Friday. Where the hell are you?'

And she realised that praying for the machine to cut him off was going to do no good at all if he was just going to call back, angrier next time. She snatched the receiver up. 'I didn't realise I was required to keep office hours.'

'Evelyn, thank God.' He blew out, long and hard and irritated, and she could almost imagine his free hand raking through his thick wavy hair in frustration. 'Where the hell have you been? I tried to call earlier.'

'I know. I heard.'

'You heard? Then why didn't you pick up? Or at least call me back?'

'Because I figured you were quite capable of searching the *Yellow Pages* yourself.'

There was a weighted pause and she heard the roar of diesel engines and hum of traffic, and she guessed he was still on the way to the hotel. 'What's that supposed to mean?'

'I mean, I'll do all manner of work for you as contracted. I'll do your correspondence and manage your diary, without issue. I'll set up appointments, do your word processing and I'll even flick off your latest girlfriend with some expensive but ultimately meaningless bauble, but don't expect me to act like some kind of pimp. As far as I recall, that wasn't one of the services I agreed to provide.'

This time the pause stretched so long she imagined the line would snap. 'Is something wrong?'

God, everything was wrong! She had appliances to replace that would suck money out of her building fund, she had a gut that was churning so hard she couldn't think straight, and now she was expected to find this man a sleeping partner. 'You're the one who left the message on my machine, remember, asking me to fix you up with a woman for the night.'

She heard a muttered curse. 'And you think I wanted you to find me someone to go to bed with.'

'What else was I supposed to think?'

'You don't think me perfectly capable of finding my own bedtime companions?'

'I would have expected so, given...' She dropped her forehead in one hand and bit down on her wayward tongue. Oh, God, what was she thinking, sparring with a client, especially when that client was almost singlehandedly funding her life and the future she was working towards? But what else could she do? It was hard to think logically with this churning gut and this tangle of barbs biting into her.

'Given what, exactly?' he prompted. 'Given the number of "expensive but ultimately meaningless baubles" I've had you send? Why, Evelyn, anyone would think you were jealous.'

I am not jealous, she wanted to argue. *I don't care who you sleep with.* But even in her own mind the words rang hollow and she could swear that the barbed wire actually laughed as it pulled tighter and pressed its pointed spines deeper into her flesh.

So, okay, maybe she had felt just a tiny bit cheated that nothing had happened that night and she hadn't ended up in his bed, but it was hardly wrong to wonder, surely? It was curiosity, more than anything. Naturally she'd had plenty of time since then to count herself lucky she had escaped that fate, after seeing how efficiently and ruthlessly he dispensed with his women, but it didn't stop her wondering what it would have been like…

She took a deep, calming breath, blew it out slowly and cursed whatever masochistic tendencies had made her pick up the phone in the first place when it would have been far more productive to rescue her washing than risk losing the best client she was ever likely to have. 'I'm sorry. Clearly I misunderstood your message. What is it that I can do for you?'

'Simple.' His liquid voice flowed down the line now she was so clearly back on task. 'I just need you to find me a wife.'

'Are you serious?'

So far this call was going nothing like he'd anticipated. It wasn't just her jumping to the wrong kind of conclusion about his earlier call that niggled at him, or her obvious disapproval of his sleeping habits—most PAs he'd met weren't that openly prudish; in fact, most he'd encountered had been too busy trying to get into his pants—but there was something else that didn't sit right about his indignant PA. She didn't sound at all like he'd expected. Admittedly he was out of practice with that demographic, but since when did middle-aged women—any woman for that matter—ask their employer if they were serious?

'Would I be asking if I weren't? And I need her in time for that dinner with Culshaw tonight. And she probably doesn't have to be a pretend wife—a pretend fiancée should do nicely.'

There was silence on the end of the line as the car climbed the sweeping approach to the Western Gate Bridge and for a moment he was almost distracted by the view of the buildings of Melbourne's sprawling CBD to his left, the port of Melbourne on his right. Until he realised they'd be at his hotel in Southbank in a matter of minutes and he needed to get things moving. He had to have tonight's arrangements squared away before he got tied up with his lunchtime meeting with the government regulators due to sign off on the transfer of ownership when it went ahead. He'd dealt with those guys before and knew it was likely to be a long lunch. 'Evelyn?'

'I'm here. Although I'm still not quite sure I understand.'

He sighed. What was so hard to understand? 'Culshaw's feeling insecure about the deal. Wants to be sure he's dealing with solid family people and, given the circumstances, maybe I don't blame him. Culshaw and Alvarez are both bringing their wives to dinner tonight, and I don't want to do anything to make Culshaw more nervous by having me turn up alone, not when we're so close to closing the deal. So I want you to increase the number at dinner to six and find me someone who can play my fiancée for a night.'

'I can certainly let the hotel know to cater for six,' she said, sounding like she meant to go on before there the line went quiet again and he sensed a 'but' coming.

'Well?' he prompted, running out of time and patience.

'I can see what you're trying to do.' Her words spilled out in a rush. 'But is taking along a pretend fiancée really wise? I mean, what if Culshaw finds out? How will that look?'

Her words grated on both his senses and his gut. Of course it was a risk, but right now, with Culshaw feeling so vulnerable, so too was turning up alone. 'Choose the right woman,' he said, 'and that won't be an issue. It's only for a night after all. Are you anywhere near your email? I sent you an idea of what I'm looking for.'

'Look, Mr Zamos—'

'Leo.'

'Okay, so, Leo, I appreciate that I got the wrong end of the stick before, but finding you someone to play fiancée, that's not exactly part of the service I offer.'

'No? Then let's make it part of them.'

'It's not actually that simple.'

'Sure it is. Find an acting school or something.

Tell whoever you find that I'm willing to pay over the odds. Have you got that email yet?'

'I'm opening it now,' she said with an air of resignation, her Australian accent softened with a hint of husky sweetness. He decided he liked it. Idly he wondered what kind of mouth it was attached to. 'Charming,' she read from the list of characteristics he'd provided, and he wondered. Surprisingly argumentative would be a better way to describe his virtual PA right now.

'Intelligent. Classy.' Again he mused. She was definitely intelligent, given the calibre of work she did for him. Classy? Maybe so if she'd worked as a corporate PA for several years. It wasn't a profession where you could get away with anything less than being impeccably groomed.

'And I've thought of something else.'

'Oh, goodie.'

Okay, so maybe charm wasn't her strong point, but so long as she got him the perfect pretend fiancée, he would overlook it for now. 'You might want to brief her on both Culshaw and Alvarez. Only the broad-brush stuff, no details. But it would be good if she wasn't completely ignorant of the players involved and what they do and can at least hold a conversation. And, of course, she'll need to know something about me as well. You know the kind of stuff…'

And then it suddenly occurred to him what had been bothering him. She said stuff like 'Are you serious?' and 'goodie' in a voice threaded with honey, and that put her age years younger than he'd expected. A glimmer of inspiration told him that if she was, maybe his search for the perfect pretend fiancée was already over…

'How old are you, Evelyn?'

'Excuse me?'

'I had you pegged for middle-aged, but you don't sound it. In fact, you sound much younger. So how old are you?'

'Is that entirely relevant right now?'

'It could be.' Though by the way she was hedging, he was pretty certain his question was unnecessary. At a guess he'd say she wasn't a day over thirty-five. It was perfect really. So perfect he was convinced it might have occurred to him earlier if he hadn't assumed his virtual PA was a good ten years older.

'And dare I ask…?' Her voice was barely a whispered breath he had to search for over the sounds of the city traffic. 'Why would that be?'

And he smiled. 'Because it would be weird if my fiancée looked old enough to be my mother.'

There was silence on the end of the line, a silence so fat with suspicion that it almost oozed out of the handset. Then that husky, hesitant Aussie drawl. 'I don't follow you.'

'It's quite simple,' he said, his blood once again fizzing with the heady buzz of a plan coming together beautifully. 'Are you doing anything for dinner tonight?'

'No. Leo—Mr Zamos. No!' This could not be happening. There was no way she was going to dinner with Leo Zamos and pretending to be his fiancée. No way!

'Excellent,' she heard him say through the mists of her panic. 'I'll have my driver pick you up at seven.'

'No! I meant yes, I'm busy. I meant no, I can't come.'

'Why? Is there a Mr Carmichael I need to smooth things over with? '

'No, but—'

'Then what's the problem?'

She squeezed her eyes shut. Tried to find the words with which to give her denial, words he might understand, before realising she didn't have to justify her position, didn't have to explain she had an infant to consider or that she didn't want to see him or that the idea simply sat uncomfortably with her. She simply had to say no. 'I don't have to do this. And neither do you, for that matter. Mr Culshaw knows you've only just flown in from overseas. Will he really be expecting you to brandish a fiancée at a business dinner?'

'But this is why it's so perfect, Evelyn. My fiancée happens to be Australian and she's already here. What could be better?'

She shook her head. For her own benefit maybe, but it made her feel better. 'It won't work. It can't. This is artifice and it will come unstuck and in grand style.'

'Evelyn,' he said measuredly, 'it can work and it will. If you let it.'

'Mr Zamos—'

'One evening, Evelyn. Just one dinner.'

'But it's not honest. We'd both be lying.'

'I prefer to think of it as offering reassurance where reassurance is needed. And if Culshaw needs reassurance before finalising this deal, who am I to deny him that?'

But making out we're engaged? 'I don't know.'

'Look, I haven't got time for this now. Let's cut to the chase. I said I was willing to pay someone above the odds and that goes for you too. This dinner is important to me, Evelyn, I don't have to tell you how much. What do you think it's worth for a few hours' work?'

'It's not about the money!'

'In my experience, it's always about the money. Shall we say ten thousand of your Australian dollars?'

Eve gasped, thinking of new clothesdryers and new hot water services and the cost of plumbers and the possibility of not dipping into her savings and still having change left over. And last but by no means least, whether Mrs Willis next door might be able to babysit tonight…

'You're right,' he said. 'Let's make it twenty. Would that be enough?'

Eve's stomach roiled, even as she felt her eyes widening in response to the temptation. 'Twenty thousand dollars,' she repeated mechanically, 'For one evening.'

'I told you it was important to me. Is it enough, do you think, to entice you to have dinner with me?'

Twenty thousand dollars enough? It didn't matter that his tone told her he was laughing at her. But for someone who had been willing to spend the night with him for nothing, the concept that he would pay so much blew her away. Did tonight really mean so much to him? Was there really that much at stake?

Really, the idea was so bizarre and ridiculous and impossible that it just might work. And, honestly, what were the chances he would recognise her? It had been almost three years ago and in a different city, and beyond heated looks they'd barely communicated that day and she doubted he even remembered her name, let alone what she looked like. And since then he'd met a thousand women in a thousand different cities, all of them beautiful, plenty of whom he'd no doubt slept with.

And since then she'd let her coloured hair settle back closer to its natural mousy colour and her body had changed with her pregnancy. Now she had curves that hadn't been there before and maybe wouldn't be there if she'd returned to work in that highly groomed, highly competitive office environment. One of the perils of working from home, she mused, was not having to keep up appearances.

Which also meant she had one hell of an afternoon in front of her if she was to be ready before seven. A glance at the wall clock told her she had less than eight hours to find a salon to squeeze into on the busiest day of the week, and find an outfit somewhere. Still assuming her neighbour could babysit tonight.

A thud came from the nursery, followed by a squeal and gurgles of pleasure, and she swung her head around. Sam was awake and busy liberating his soft toys from the confines of the cot. That meant she had about thirty seconds before he was the last man left standing and demanding to be released from jail the way he knew best. The loud way.

'There's a couple of things I have to square away,' she said, anxious to get off the phone before Sam decided to howl the place down. 'Can I call you back in a few minutes to confirm?'

'Of course,' he said, in that velvet-rich voice that felt like it was stroking her. 'Call me. So long as it's a yes.'

Leo slipped his phone into his pocket as the car came to a smooth halt outside his hotel. A door-man touched his gloved fingers to his hat as he pulled open the door, bowing his welcome. 'We've been expecting you, Mr Zamos.' He handed him a slim pink envelope that bore his name and a room number on the front. 'Your suite is ready if you'd like to go straight up.'

'Excellent,' he said, nodding his thanks as he strode into the hotel entry and headed for the lifts, feeling more and more confident by the minute. He'd known Evelyn would soon have that little problem sorted, although maybe he hadn't exactly anticipated her sorting it so quickly and efficiently.

What was she like? he wondered as the lift whisked him soundlessly skywards. Was he wrong not to insist on a photo of her to be safe? Originally he'd had looks on his list of requirements, on the basis that if he had to act as someone's fiancé, he'd expected it would be one hell of a lot easier to be act the part if he didn't have to force himself to smile whenever he looked at her or slipped his arm around her shoulders. But maybe someone more ordinary would be more convincing. Culshaw didn't strike him as the sort of man who went for looks over substance and, given his circumstances, he'd be looking for a love match in the people he did business with. In which case, some nice plain girl might just fit the bill.

It was only for one night, after all.

The lift doors whooshed open on the twenty-fourth floor onto a window with a view over the outer city that stretched to the sea and air faintly scented with ginger flower.

Other than to get his bearings, he paid scant

attention to the view. It was success Leo Zamos could smell first and foremost, success that set his blood to fizzing as he headed for his suite.

God, but he loved it when a plan came together!

CHAPTER THREE

EVE had some idea of how Cinderella must have felt on her way to the ball. Half an hour ago she'd left her old world behind, all tumbling-down house and broken-down appliances and baby rusks, and was now being whisked off in a silken gown to a world she had only ever dreamt of.

Had Cinderella been similarly terrified on her way to the ball? Had she felt this tangle of nerves writhing in her stomach as she'd neared the palace on that fairy-tale night? Had she felt this cold, hard fear that things would come terribly, terribly unstuck before the night was over? If so, she could well empathise.

Not that her story was any kind of fairy-tale. There'd been no fairy godmother who could transform her into some kind of princess in an instant with a touch of her magic wand for a start. Instead, Eve had spent the afternoon in a blur of preparations, almost spinning from salon to boutiques to appliance stores, in between packing up tiny pots of yoghurt and Sam's favourite pasta so Mrs Willis wouldn't have to worry about finding him something to eat. There had been no time for reflection, no time to sit down and really think about what she was doing or why she was even doing it.

But here, sitting alone against the buttery-soft upholstery of an entire limousine, she had no distractions, no escape from asking herself the questions that demanded to be answered. Why was she doing this? Why had she agreed to be Leo's pretend fiancée, when all her instincts told her it was wrong? Why hadn't she insisted on saying no?

Sure, there was the money. She wouldn't call herself mercenary exactly, but she was motivated at the thought of getting enough money together to handle both her renovations and taking care of Sam. And how else would she so quickly gather the funds to replace a hot water service that had inconsiderately died twelve months too early and buy a new clothesdryer so she could keep up with Sam's washing in the face of Melbourne's fickle weather?

What other reason could there be?

Because you're curious.

Ridiculous. She thrust the suggestion aside, determined to focus on the view. She loved Melbourne. After so many years in Sydney, it was good to be home, not that she got into the city too often these days.

But the annoying, niggling voice in her head refused to be captivated or silenced by the view.

You want to see if he has the same impact on you that he had three years ago.

You want to know if it's not just his voice that makes your stomach curl.

You want to know if he'll once again look at you with eyes filled with dark desire and simmering need.

No, no and no! She shuffled restlessly against the leather, adjusting her seat belt so it wasn't so tight across her chest and she could breathe easier.

Dark desire and simmering need were the last

things she needed these days. She had responsibilities now. A child to provide for. Which was exactly what she was doing by coming tonight, she acknowledged, latching onto the concept with zeal. She was providing for her child. After all, if she didn't, who would? Not his father, that was for sure.

She bit down on her lip, remembering only then that she was wearing lipstick for a change and that she shouldn't do that. It had been harder than she'd imagined, leaving Sam for an evening—the first time she'd ever left him at night—and it had been such a wrench she'd been almost tempted to call Leo and tell him she'd changed her mind.

But she hadn't. And Sam had splashed happily in an early bath and enjoyed dinner. She'd read him a story and he'd already been nodding off when she'd left him with Mrs Willis, his little fist clenched, his thumb firmly wedged between cupid bow lips. But what if he woke up and she wasn't there? What if he wouldn't settle back down for Mrs Willis?

God, what the hell had she been thinking, agreeing to this?

Outside the limousine windows the city of Melbourne was lighting up. It wasn't long after seven, the sky caught in that time between day and night, washed with soft shadows that told of the coming darkness, and buildings were preparing, showing their colours, strutting their stuff.

Just like she was, she thought. She wore a gown of aqua silk, which had cost her the equivalent of a month's salary in her old office job, but she figured the evening called for something more grand than her usual chain-store purchases. Leo would no doubt expect it, she figured. And she'd loved the dress as she'd slipped it over her head and zipped it up, loved the look of it over her post-baby curves and the feel of it against her skin, and loved what it did to accentuate the colour of her eyes, but the clincher had been when her eighteen-month-old son had looked up at her from his pram, broken into an enormous grin and clapped his pudgy hands together.

And she must look all right in her new dress and newly highlighted hair because her neighbour had gasped when she'd come to the door to deliver Sam and insisted she cover herself with an apron in case she inadvertently spilled anything on it before she left.

Dear Mrs Willis, who was the closest to a grandparent that Sam would ever know, and who had been delighted to babysit and have Eve go out for a night for a change, no doubt in the hope that Eve would find a nice man to settle down with and provide a father to Sam. And even though Eve had explained it was a work function and she'd no doubt be home early, her neighbour had simply smiled and taken no notice as she'd practically pushed her out the door to the waiting car. 'Have a lovely evening and don't rush. If it's after ten when you get home, I'll no doubt be asleep, so you can come and pick Sam up in the morning.'

And then they were there. The driver pulled into a turnaround and eased the car to a stop. He passed her a keycard as a doorman stepped forward to open her door. 'Mr Zamos says to let you know he's running late and to let yourself in.' She smiled her thanks as he recited a room number, praying she'd manage to remember it as the doorman welcomed her to the hotel.

Deep breath.

Warily she stepped out of the car, cautious on heels that seemed perilously high, where once upon a time she would have thought nothing of sprinting to catch a bus in even higher. Strange, what skills you forgot, she thought, when you don't use them. And then she sincerely hoped she hadn't forgotten the art of making conversation with adults because a few rounds of 'Open, shut them, open, shut them,' was going to get tired pretty quickly.

And then she stepped through the sliding doors into the hotel and almost turned around and walked straight back out again. It was little more than the entrance, a bank of grand elevators in front of her and a lift lobby to the left, but it was beautiful. A massive arrangement of flowers sat between the escalators, lilies bright and beautiful, palm leaves vivid green and all so artfully arranged that it looked too good to be real.

Just like her, she thought. Because she did so not belong here in this amazing place. She was a fake, pretending to be something she was not, and everyone would see through her in an instant.

She must have hesitated too long or maybe they recognised her as a fraud because someone emerged from behind the concierge desk and asked if she needed assistance. 'I'm to meet Mr Zamos in his suite,' she said, her voice sounding other-worldy in the moneyed air of one of Melbourne's most prestigious hotels, but instead of calling for Security, like she half expected, he simply led her to the lift lobby and saw her safely inside a lift, even smiling as he pressed Leo's level on the floor selection so she could make no mistake.

Oh, God, she thought, clutching her shawl around her as the lift door pinged open on the chosen floor, the keycard clenched tightly in her fingers, this is it.

One night, she told herself, it's just one night. *One evening*, she corrected herself, *just a dinner*. Because in just a few short hours she would be home and life could get back to normal and she could go back to being a work-from-home mum in her trackpants again.

She could hardly wait.

She stepped out into the lift lobby, drinking

deeply of the hotel's sweetly spiced air, willing it to give her strength as she started on the long journey down the hall. Her stomach felt alive with the beating of a thousand tiny wings, giving flight to a thousand tiny and not so tiny fears and stopping her feet dead on the carpet.

What the hell was she doing? How could she be so sure Leo wouldn't recognise her? And how could she bear it if he did? The shame of knowing how she'd acted—like some kind of wanton. How could she possibly keep working for him if he knew?

Because she wasn't like that. Not normally. A first date might end with a kiss if it had gone well, the concept of a one-night stand the furthest thing from her mind, but something about Leo had stripped away her usual cautiousness, turning her reckless, wanting it all and wanting it now.

She couldn't bear it if he knew. She couldn't bear the aftermath or the subsequent humiliation.

Would he terminate her contract?

Or would he expect to pick up where he'd left off?

She shivered, her thumping heart beating much too loud for the hushed, elegant surroundings.

Lift doors pinged softly behind her and she glanced around as a couple emerged from the lift, forcing her to move both her feet and her thoughts closer to Leo's door.

Seriously, why should he remember her? A rushed grope in a filing room with a woman he hadn't seen before or since. Clearly it would mean nothing to a man with such an appetite for sex. He'd probably forgotten her the moment he'd left the building. And she'd been Eve then, too. Not the Evelyn she'd reverted to when she'd started her virtual PA business, wanting to sound serious and no-nonsense on her website.

And it's only one night, she told herself, willing herself to relax as she arrived at the designated door. Just one short evening. And then she looked down at the keycard in her damp hand and found she'd been clenching it so tightly it had bitten deep and left bold white lines across her fingers.

Let herself in when it was the last place she wanted to be? Hardly. She rapped softly on the door. Maybe the driver was wrong. Maybe he wasn't even there…

There was no answer, even after a second knock, so taking a fortifying breath she slid the card through the reader. There was a whirr and click and a green light winked at her encouragingly.

The door swung open to a large sitting room decorated in soft toffee and cream tones. 'Hello,' she ventured softly, snicking the door closed behind her, not game to venture yet beyond the entryway other than to admire the room and its elegant furnishings. Along the angled wall sat a sofa with chairs arranged around a low coffee table, while opposite a long dresser bore a massive flatscreen television. A desk faced the window, a laptop open on top. Through the open door alongside, she could just make out the sound of someone talking.

Leo, if the way her nerves rippled along her spine was any indication. And then the voice grew less indistinct and louder and she heard him say, 'I've got the figures right here. Hang on…'

A moment later he strode into the room without so much as a glance in her direction, all his focus on the laptop that flashed into life with just a touch, while all her focus was on him clad in nothing more than a pair of black silk briefs that made nothing more than a passing concession to modesty.

He was a god, from the tips of his damp tousled hair all the way down, over broad muscled shoulders that flexed as he moved his hand over the keyboard, over olive skin that glistened under the light, and over the tight V of his hips to the tapered muscular legs below.

And Eve felt muscles clench that she hadn't even known she'd possessed.

She must have made some kind of sound—she hoped to God it wasn't a whimper—because he stilled and glanced at the window in front of him, searching the reflection. She knew the instant he saw her, knew it in the way his muscles stiffened, his body straightening before he slowly turned around, his eyes narrowing as they drank her in, so measuredly, so heatedly she was sure they must leave tracks on her skin.

'I'll call you back,' he said into the phone, without taking his eyes from her, without making any attempt to leave the room or cover himself. 'Something's come up.'

She risked a glance—*there*—and immediately wished she hadn't, for when she looked back at him, his eyes glinted knowingly, the corners creasing, as if he'd known exactly what she'd been doing and where she'd been looking.

'Evelyn?'

He was waiting for an answer, but right now her tongue felt like it was stuck to the roof of her mouth, her softly fitted dress seemed suddenly too tight, too restrictive, and the man opposite her was too big and all too obviously virile. And much, much too undressed. The fact he made no attempt to cover himself up only served to unsettle her even more.

He took a step closer. 'You're Evelyn Carmichael?'

She took a step back. 'You were expecting someone else?'

'No. Nobody else—except…'

'Except what?' she whispered, wondering if

spiders' eyes glinted the same way his did as they sized up their prey.

'I sure as hell wasn't expecting anyone like you.'

She felt dizzy, unbalanced and unprepared, and there was absolutely no question in her mind what she had to do next, no wavering. She turned, one hand already fumbling for the door handle, her nails scratching against the wood. 'Clearly you're not ready,' she said, breathless and panicky and desperate to escape. 'I'll wait outside.'

But she'd barely pulled it open an inch before a hand pushed it closed over her shoulder. 'There's no need to run away.'

No need? Who was he trying to kid? What about the fact a near-naked man was standing a bare few inches away from her and filling the air she breathed with a near-fatal mix of soap and citrus and pure, unadulterated testosterone? A man she'd once been prepared to spend the night with, a lost night she'd fantasised about ever since. A man standing so close she could feel his warm breath fanning the loose ends of her hair, sending warm shivers down her neck. What more reason did a girl need to flee?

Apart from the knowledge that it wasn't the beast she had to be afraid of after all. It wasn't the beast she couldn't trust.

It was her own unquenched desires.

'Stay. Help yourself to something from the minibar while I get dressed next door. I promise I won't be long.'

'Thanks,' she whispered softly to the door, not sure if she was thanking him for the offer of a drink or for the fact he was intending to put some clothes on. But she was sure about not turning around before he removed his arm from over her shoulder and moved away. Far, far away with any luck. 'I'll do that.'

And then the arm withdrew and she sensed the air shift and swirl as he departed, leaving her feeling strangely bereft instead of relieved, like she'd expected. Bereft and embarrassed. God, she must seem so unsophisticated and gauche compared to the usual kind of woman he entertained, practically bolting from the room with her cheeks on fire like some schoolgirl who'd wandered into the wrong loos by mistake!

She could actually do with a stiff drink right now, she mused, still shaky as she pulled open the minibar fridge, assuming she could open her throat wide enough to drink it. Then again, tonight would be a very good night not to drink alcohol, and not just because she probably had no tolerance for it these days. But because drinking anything with anaesthetic qualities in this man's presence would be a very, very bad idea.

Especially given she was already half-intoxicated just being in his presence.

True to his word, he was already returning from the room beyond by the time she'd made her selection, a pair of slim-fitting black trousers encasing those powerful-looking legs and a crisp white shirt buttoned over his broad chest. Even dressed, he still looked like a god rather than any mere mortal, tall, dynamic and harshly beautiful, and yet for one insane, irrational moment her eyes actually mourned the loss of naked skin to feast upon, until he joined her at the minibar and it occurred to her that at least now she might be able to speak coherently.

'Did you find something?' he asked, as she moved aside to give him room as he pulled a beer from the fridge.

'Yes, thanks,' she said, twisting the cap from a bottle of mineral water and grabbing a glass, still discomfited by his presence. Then again, it was impossible to see him clothed and not think about those broad shoulders, the pebbled nipples and the cluster of dark hair between them that swirled like storm fronts on a weather map, before heading south, circling his navel and arrowing still downwards...

She sucked in a rush of air, cursing when it came once again laced with his tell-tale scent. Distance was what she needed and soon, and she took advantage of his phone ringing again to find it. She did a quick risk assessment of the sitting room and decided an armchair was the safest option. She needed to stop thinking about Leo Zamos with no clothes on and start thinking about something else. Something that didn't return the flush to her skin and the heat to her face.

Like the decor. Her eyes latched onto a trip-tych set above the sofa. Perfect. The three black and white prints featured photographs of Melbourne street-scapes from the Fifties and Six-ties, their brushed gold frames softening their impact against the cream-coloured wall. Under-stated. Tasteful. Like the rest of the furnishings, she thought, drinking in the elegant surrounds of the sitting area and admiring how the decorator had so successfully combined a mix of fabrics, patterns and textures. Maybe she should try for something similar…

And then Leo finished the call and dropped onto the sofa opposite, scuttling every thought in her head. He stretched one arm out along the top of the cushions, crossed one long leg over the other and took a swig from his beer, all the while studying her until her skin prickled with the intensity of his gaze and her heart cranked up in her chest till she was afraid to breathe.

'It's a pleasure to meet you, Evelyn Carmichael, my virtual PA. I have to say I'm delighted to find you're very much real and not so virtual after all.' And then he shook his head slowly and

Eve's lungs shut down on the panicked thought, *He knows*! Except his mouth turned up into a wry smile. 'Why did I ever imagine you were middle-aged?'

And breath whooshed from her lungs, so relieved she even managed a smile. 'Not quite yet, thankfully.'

'But your credentials—your CV was a mile long. What did you do, leave school when you were ten?'

The question threw her, amazed he'd remembered the details she'd supplied when he'd first sent his enquiry through her website. But better he remember those details rather than a frenetic encounter in a filing room with a PA with a raging libido. 'I was seventeen. I did my commercial degree part time. I was lucky enough to make a few good contacts and get head-hunted to a few high-end roles.'

His eyes narrowed again and she could almost see the cogs turning inside his head. 'Surely that's every PA's dream. What made you leave all that and go out on your own? It must have been a huge risk.'

'Oh, you know…' she said, her hands fluttering around her glass. 'Just things. I'd been working in an office a long time and…'

'And?'

And I got pregnant to one of the firm's inter-state consultants…

She shrugged. 'It was time for a change.'

He leaned forward, held out his beer towards her in a toast. 'Well, the bricks and mortar office world's loss is my gain. It's a pleasure meeting you at last after all this time, Evelyn. You don't know how much of a pleasure it is.'

They touched drinks, her glass against his bottle, his bottomless eyes not leaving hers for a moment, and now she'd reeled in her panic, she remembered the heat and the sheer power of that gaze and the way it could find a place deep down inside her that seemed to unfurl and blossom in the warmth.

'And you,' she murmured, taking a sip of her sparkling water, needing the coolness against her heated skin, tempted to hold the glass up to her burning cheeks.

Nothing had changed, she thought as the cooling waters slid down her throat. Leo Zamos was still the same. Intense, powerful, and as dangerous as sin.

And it was no consolation to learn that after everything she'd been through these last few years, everything she'd learned, she was just as affected, just as vulnerable.

No consolation at all.

She was perfect. Absolutely perfect. He sipped his beer and reflected on the list of qualities he'd wanted in a pretend fiancée as he watched the woman sitting opposite him, trying so hard to look at ease as she perched awkwardly on the edge of her seat, picking up her glass and then putting it down, forgetting to drink from it before picking it up again and going through the same nervous ritual before she excused herself to use the powder room.

She'd been so reluctant to come tonight. What was that about when clearly she ticked every box? She was intelligent, he knew that for a fact given the calibre of the work she did for him. And that dress and that classically upswept hair spoke of class, nothing cheap or tacky there.

As for charming, he'd never seen anything as charming as the way she'd blushed, totally mortified when confronted by his state of undress before she'd tried to flee from the room. He'd had no idea she was there or he would never have scared her like that, but, then, how long had it been since a woman had run the other way when they'd seen him without his clothes on? Even room service the world over weren't that precious, and yet she'd taken off like the devil himself had been after her. What was her problem? It wasn't like he was a complete stranger to her after all. Then again, she'd made plain her disapproval of his long line of companions. Maybe she was scared she might end up on it.

Now, there was a thought...

He discounted the idea as quickly as it had come. She was his PA after all, even if a virtual one, and a rule was a rule. Maybe a shame, on reflection, that he'd made that rule, but he'd made it knowing he might be tempted from time to time and he'd made it for good reason. But at least he knew he wouldn't have to spend the night forcing himself to smile at a woman he wasn't interested in. He found it easy to smile at her now, as she returned from the powder room, coyly avoiding his eyes. She was uncannily, serendipitously perfect, from the top of her honey-caramel hair to the tips of the lacquered toenails peeping out of her shoes. And he had to smile. To think he'd imagined her middle-aged and taking nanna naps! How wrong could a man be? He would have no trouble at all feigning interest in this woman, no trouble at all.

He rose, heading her off before she could sit down, her eyes widening as he approached and blocked off the route to her armchair so she was forced to stop, even in heels forced to tilt her head up to look at him. Even now her colour was unnaturally high, her bright eyes alert as if she was poised on the brink of escape.

There was no chance of escape.

Oh no. His clever, classy little virtual PA wasn't going anywhere yet. Not before he'd convinced Culshaw that he had nothing to fear from dealing with him, and that he was a rock-solid family man. Which meant he just had to convince Evelyn that she had nothing to fear from him.

'Are we late?' she asked, sounding breathless and edgy. 'Is it time to go?'

He could be annoyed at her clear display of nerves. He should be if her nervousness put his plans at risk. But somehow the entire package was so enticing. He liked it that he so obviously affected her. And so what that she wasn't plain? She wasn't exactly classically pretty either—her green eyes were perhaps too wide, her nose too narrow, but they were balanced by a wide mouth that lent itself to both the artist's paintbrush and to thoughts of long afternoons of lazy sex.

Not necessarily in that order.

For just one moment he thought he'd noted those precise details in a face before, but the snatch of memory was fleeting, if in fact it was memory at all, and flittered away before he could pin it down to a place or time. No matter. Nothing mattered right now but that she was there and that he had a good feeling about tonight. His lips curved into a smile. A very good feeling.

'Not yet. Dinner is set for eight in the presidential suite.'

She glanced at the sparkly evening watch on her wrist and then over her shoulder, edging ever so slightly towards the door, and as much as he found her agitation gratifying, he knew he had to sort this out. 'Maybe I should check with the staff that everything's good with the dinner,' she suggested. 'Just remind them that it's for a party of six now...'

He shook his head benevolently, imagining this was how gamekeepers felt when they soothed nervous animals. 'Evelyn, it's all under control. Besides, there's something more important you should be doing right now.' He touched the pad of his middle finger, just one finger, to her shoulder and she jumped and shrank back.

'And what might that be?' she asked, breathless and trembling and trying to mask it by feigning interest in the closest photographic print on the wall. A picture of the riverbank, he noticed with a glance, of trees and park benches and some old man sitting in the middle of the bench, gazing out at the river. That wouldn't hold her attention for long. Not when he did this…

'You're perfect,' he said, lifting his hand to a stray tendril of hair that had come loose and feeling her shudder as his fingertips caressed her neck. 'I couldn't have asked for a better pretend fiancée.'

Her eyelids fluttered as he swore she swayed into his touch until she seemed to snap herself awake and shift the other way. 'I sense a "but" coming.'

'No buts,' he said, pretending to focus on the print on the wall before them. 'We just have to get our stories straight, in case someone asks us how we met. I was thinking it would make sense to keep things as close to the truth as possible. That you were working as my PA and one thing led to another.'

'I guess.'

'And we've been together now, what, two years? Except we don't see each other that often as I'm always on the move and you live in Australia.'

'That makes sense.'

'That makes perfect sense. And explains why we want to wait before making that final commitment.'

'Marriage.' She nodded. 'We're taking our time.'

'Exactly,' he said, slipping a tentative arm around her shoulders, feeling her shudder at the contact. 'We want to be absolutely sure, which is hard when we only get to see each other a few snatched times a year.'

'Okay. I've got that.'

'Excellent.' He turned towards her. Put a finger under her chin and lifted it so that she had no choice but to look into his eyes. 'But there's one thing you don't get.'

'I knew there was a but coming,' she said, and he would have laughed, but she was so nervous, so on edge, and he didn't want to spook her. Not when she was so important to him tonight.

'This one's simple,' he said. 'All you have to do is relax with me.'

'I'm perfectly relaxed,' she said stiffly, sounding more like a prim librarian than any kind of lover.

'Are you, when my slightest touch…' he ran a fingertip down her arm and she shivered and shied away '…clearly makes you uncomfortable.'

'It's a dinner,' she said, defensively. 'Why should you need to touch me?'

'Because any red-blooded man, especially one intending to marry you and who doesn't get the chance to see you that often, would want to touch you every possible moment of every day.'

'Oh.'

'Oh, indeed. You see my problem.'

'So what do you suggest?'

Her eyes were wide and luminous and up close he could see they were neither simply green nor blue but all the myriad colours of the sea mixed together, the vibrant green where the shallow water kissed the sand, the sapphire blue of the deep water, and everything in between. And even though she was supposed to be off limits, he found himself wondering what they'd look like when she came.

'I find practice usually makes perfect.'

She swallowed, and he followed the movement

down her slender throat. 'You want to practise touching me?'

Fascinated, his thumb found the place where the movement had disappeared, his fingers tracing her collarbone and feeling her trembling response, before sliding around her neck, drawing her closer as his eyes settled on her too-wide lips, deciding they weren't too wide at all, but as close to perfect as they could get.

'And I want you to practise not jumping every time I do.'

'I…I'll try,' she said, a mist rolling in over her eyes, and he doubted she even realised she was already swaying into his touch.

He smiled as he tilted her chin with his other hand, his thumb stroking along the line of her jaw. 'You see, it's not that hard.'

She blinked, looking confused. 'I understand. I…I'll be fine.'

But he had no intention of ending the lesson yet. Not when he had such a willing and biddable pupil. 'Excellent,' he said, tilting her chin higher, 'and now there's just one more thing.'

'There is?' she breathed.

'Of course,' he said, once again drawing her closer, his eyes once again on her lips. 'We just need to get that awkward first kiss out of the way.'

CHAPTER FOUR

SHE barely had time to gasp, barely had time to think before his lips brushed hers, so feather-light in their touch, so devastating in their impact that she trembled against him, thankful for both his solidity and his strength.

More thankful when his lips returned, this time to linger, to play about her mouth, teasing and coaxing and stealing the air from her lungs.

She heard a sound—a mewl of pleasure—and realised it had emanated from the depths of her own desperate need.

Realised she was clinging to him, her fingers anchored in his firm-fleshed shoulders.

Realised that either or both of these things had triggered something in Leo, for suddenly his kiss deepened, his mouth more punishing, and she was swept away on a wave of sensation like she'd only ever experienced once before. He was everywhere, his taste in her mouth, his hot breath on her cheek, his scent filling the air she breathed.

And the feel of his steel-like arms around her, his hard body plastered against her, was almost too much to comprehend, too much to absorb.

It was too much to think. It was enough to kiss and be kissed, to feel the probing exploration of his tongue, the invitation to tangle and dance, and accept that intimate invitation.

How many nights had she remembered the power of this kiss, remembered what it felt like to be held in Leo's arms? It had been her secret fantasy, fuelled by one heated encounter with a stranger, but even she had not recalled this utter madness, this sheer frantic expression of need.

It was everything she'd ever dreamed of and more, that chance to recapture these feelings. And then he shifted to drop his mouth to her throat and she felt him, rock hard against her belly, and she shuddered hard against him, a shudder that intensified as he skimmed his hands up her sides and brushed peaked nipples in ach-ingly full breasts with electric thumbs.

She groaned as his lips returned to her mouth, a feather-light kiss that lasted a fraction of a second before the air shifted and swirled cold around her and he was gone.

She opened her eyes, breathless and stunned and wondering what had just happened. 'Excellent,' he said thickly. 'That should do nicely. Wait here. I've got something for you.' He turned and disappeared into the other room. She slumped against the credenza behind her, put her hands to her face and tried not to think about how she'd responded to his kiss exactly like she had the first time. Drugged stupid with desire, shameless in her response to him.

Excellent? Hardly. Not when in another ten seconds he could have had her dress off. Another twenty and she would probably have ripped it off herself in desperation to save him the trouble. And all because he didn't want her to be nervous around him! God, how was she supposed to be anything but, especially after that little performance? Had she learned nothing in the intervening years?

She'd barely managed to catch her breath when

Leo returned, a tie looped loosely around his collar, a jacket over his arm, and an expression she couldn't quite read on his face. Not the smug satisfaction she'd expected, but something that looked almost uncomfortable. When she saw the two small boxes in his hand, she thought she knew why and she didn't feel any better.

'Try these on,' he said, offering the boxes to her. 'I borrowed them for the night. Hopefully one should fit well enough.'

'You borrowed them?' she said, considering them warily, knowing what came in dangerous-looking little blue boxes like those. And if his words were a hint that whatever sparkly bauble she would wear on her finger wouldn't be hers to keep, it wasn't terribly subtle. But that wasn't what bothered her. Rather, it was the artifice of it all, like they were gilding the lie, layering pretence upon pretence. 'Is this strictly necessary?'

He lifted her hand, dropped the boxes on her palm. 'They'll notice if you don't wear an engagement ring.'

'Can't I simply be your girlfriend?'

'Fiancée sounds much better. All that added

commitment.' He winked as he shrugged into his jacket. 'Besides, I've already told them. Go on, try them on.'

Reluctantly she opened the first. Brilliant light erupted from the stone, a huge square-cut diamond set in a sculpted white-gold band, inlaid with tiny pink diamonds. She couldn't imagine anything more stunning.

Until she opened the second and imagination took a back seat to reality. It was magnificent, a Ceylon sapphire set with diamonds either side. She had never seen anything so beautiful. Certainly had never imagined wearing anything as beautiful. She put down the box with the white-gold ring, tugged the other ring free and slipped it on her finger, hoping—*secretly praying*—that it would fit, irrationally delighted when it skimmed over her knuckle and nestled perfectly at the base of her finger.

She looked down at her hand, turning it this way and that, watching the blue lights dance in the stone. 'They must be worth a fortune.'

He shrugged, as if it was no matter, using the mirror to deftly negotiate the two ends of his tie into a neat knot. 'A small one, perhaps. It's not like I'm actually buying them.'

'No. Of course not.' He was merely borrowing them for a night to help convince people he was getting married. Just like he was borrowing her.

But even his ruthless designs couldn't stop her wondering what it must be like to be given such a ring, such an object of incredible beauty, by the man you loved? To have him slide that ring on your finger to the sound of a heartfelt 'I love you. Marry me,' instead of, *'Go on, try them on'.*

The sapphire caught the light, its polished facets throwing a dozen different shades of blue, the diamonds sparkling, and she felt her resistance wavering.

With or without the ring, she was already pretending to be something she was not. Could she really make the lie worse than it already was?

'Very nice,' he said, lifting her fingers. 'Have you tried the other one?'

She looked down at the open box, and the pale beauty that resided there. 'No real need,' she said, trying to sound like she didn't care as well as make out that she wasn't bothered by his proximity, even though her fingers tingled and her body buzzed with his closeness. 'This one fits perfectly.'

'And it matches your eyes.'

She looked up to see him studying her face. 'You know you have the most amazing eyes, every shade of the sea and more.'

'Th-thank you.'

He lifted a hand to her face and swiped the pad of his thumb at the corner of her mouth. 'And you have a little smudge of lipstick right here.' He smiled a knowing smile. 'How did that happen, I wonder?'

Instinctively she put a hand over her mouth, backing away. 'I better repair my make-up,' she said, sweeping up her evening purse from the coffee table and making for the powder room. How had that happened indeed. She really didn't need to be reminded of that kiss and how she'd practically given him a green light to do whatever he wanted with her. It was amazing it was only her lipstick that had slipped. Well, there would be no more smudged lipstick if she had any say in it. None at all.

He watched her go, his eyes missing nothing of her ramrod-straight spine or the forced stiffness that hampered her movements. She hadn't been stiff or hampered a few moments ago, when she'd all but rested her cheek against his hand. She hadn't been stiff or hampered when he'd held her in his arms and kissed her senseless.

'Evelyn,' he called behind her, and she stopped and turned, gripping her purse tightly in front of her chest. 'Something that might make you feel more relaxed in my company...'

'Yes?' She sounded sceptical.

'As much as I enjoyed that kiss, I have a rule about not mixing business with pleasure.'

She blinked those big blue eyes up at him and he could tell she didn't get it. 'I don't sleep with my PA. Whatever I do tonight, a touch, a caress, a kiss, it's all just part of an act. You're perfectly safe with me. All right?'

And something—he'd expected relief, but it wasn't quite that—flashed across her eyes and was gone. 'Of course,' she said, and fled into to powder room.

There. He'd said it. He blew out a breath as he

picked up the leftover ring from the coffee table, snapped the box shut and returned it to the safe. Maybe it was, as he had said, to put her at her ease, but there'd also been a measure of wanting to remind himself of his golden rule. Because it had been hard enough to remember which way was up, let alone anything else in the midst of that kiss.

He hadn't intended it to go so far. He'd meant to tease her into submission, give her just a little taste for more, so she'd be more malleable and receptive to his touch, but she'd sighed into his mouth and turned molten and turned him incendiary with it.

And if he hadn't frightened her away by the strength of his reaction, he'd damned near frightened himself. He'd had to leave the room before she could see how affected he was, and before he looked into her ocean-deep eyes and decided to finish what he'd started.

He ached to finish what he'd started.

Why did he have that rule about not sleeping with his PAs? What had he been thinking? Surely this was a matter that should be decided on a case-by-case basis.

And then he remembered Inge of the ice-cool demeanour and red hot bedroom athletics and how she'd so neatly tried to demand a chunk of ice for her finger by nailing him with her alleged pregnancy.

There was good reason for his self-imposed rule, he reluctantly acknowledged. Damn good reason.

If only he could make himself believe it.

She didn't recognise herself in the powder-room mirror. Even after repairing her make-up and smoothing the stray wisps of her hair back into its sleek coil, she still looked like a stranger. No amount of lipstick could disguise the flush to her swollen lips. And while the ring on her finger sparkled under the light, it was no match for the lights in her eyes.

Not when all she could do was remember that kiss, and how he had damn near wrenched out her mind if not her soul with it.

It was wrong to feel excited, even though its

impact had so closely mirrored that of the first. But he'd simply been making a point. He'd been acting. He'd said as much himself. It had meant nothing. Or else why could he so easily have turned and walked away?

Yet still she trembled at the memory of his lips on hers. Still she trembled when she thought of how he'd felt, pressing hard and insistent against her belly, stirring secret places until they blossomed and ached with want.

Want that would go unsatisfied. Cheated again. Just an act. *'I don't sleep with my PA.'*

And part of her had longed to laugh and tell him that he'd had his chance, years ago, and blown it then. Another part had wanted to slump with relief. While the greater part of her had wanted to protest at the unfairness of it all.

Damn. She'd known this would be difficult. She'd known that seeing him again would rekindle all those feelings she had been unable to bury, unable to dim, even with the passage of time.

She dragged air into her lungs, breathed out slowly and resolutely angled her chin higher as she made one final check on her appearance. For surely the worst was over. And at least she knew where she stood. She may as well try to enjoy the rare evening out.

How hard could it be?

'Remember,' Leo said, as they made their way to the presidential suite, 'keep it light and friendly and whatever you do, avoid any talk of family.'

Suits me, she thought, knowing Leo would be less than impressed if she started telling everyone about Sam. 'What is it exactly that their sons are supposed to have done?'

'You didn't see the articles?'

She shook her head. 'Clearly I don't read the right kind of magazine.'

'Or visit the right websites. Someone got a video of them at a party and posted it on the web.'

'And they were doing something embarrass-ing?'

'You could say that. It was a wife-swapping party.'

'Oh.'

'Oh, indeed. Half the board were implicated

and Culshaw couldn't stand seeing what he'd worked for all his life being dragged through the mud.' He stopped outside the suite. 'Are you ready?'

As ready as I'll ever be. 'Yes.'

He slipped her hand into his, surprising her but not so much this time because it was unexpected but because it felt so comfortable to have his large hand wrapped around hers. Amazing, given the circumstances, that it felt so right. 'You look beautiful,' he whispered, so close to her ear that she could feel his warm breath kiss her skin, setting light to her senses and setting flame licking at her core.

It's make-believe, she warned herself as he tilted her chin and she once more gave herself up to his kiss, this time a kiss so tender and sweet that the very air seemed to shimmer and spin like gold around her. She drew herself back, trying to find logic in a sea of sensation and air that didn't come charged with the spice of him.

It meant nothing, a warning echoed as he pressed the buzzer. It was all just part of the act.

She could not afford to start thinking it felt right. She could not afford to think it was real.

She had just one short evening of pretending this man loved her and she loved him, and then the make-believe ended and she could go home to her falling-down house and her baby son. Alone. That was reality. That was her life.

She should be grateful it was so easy to pretend…

A butler opened the door, showing them into an impressive mirror-lined entry that opened into the massive presidential suite, Eve's heels clicked on the high gloss parquet floor. Floor-to-ceiling mirrors either side reflected their images back at them, and Eve was struck when she realised that the woman in that glamorous couple, her hand in Leo's and her eyes still sparkling, was her. Maybe she shouldn't feel so nervous. Maybe they could pull this off. It had seemed such a crazy idea, and questions remained in her mind as to the ethics of the plan, but maybe they could convince his business colleagues they were a couple. Certainly she had twenty thousand good reasons to try.

'Welcome, welcome!' An older man came to

meet them and Eve recognised him from the newspapers. Eric Culshaw had aged, though, she noticed, his silvering hair white at the temples, his shoulders a little stooped as if he'd held the weight of the world on them. Given the nature of the scandal that had rocked his world, maybe that was how he felt. He pumped Leo's hand. 'Welcome to you both,' he said, smiling broadly.

'Eric,' Leo said, 'allow me to introduce my fiancée, Evelyn Carmichael.'

And Eric's smile widened as he took her hand. 'It is indeed a pleasure, Evelyn. Come over and meet everyone.'

Eve needed the few short seconds to get over the scale of the suite. She'd arranged the bookings for all the rooms, similar corner spa suites for Leo and the Alvarezes, and the presidential suite for the Culshaws, but she'd had no idea just how grand they were. Leo's suite had seemed enormous, with the separate living area, but this suite was more like an entire home. A dining room occupied the right third of the room, a study opposite the entry, and to the left a generous sitting area, filled with plump sofas and welcoming armchairs. Doors hinted at still more rooms, no doubt lavish bedrooms and bathrooms and a kitchen for the dining room, and all along one side was a wall of windows to take in the view of the Melbourne city skyline. The others were sipping champagne in the living room, admiring the view, when they joined them.

Eric made the introductions. Maureen Culshaw was a slim sixty-something with a pinched face, like someone had pricked her bubble when she wasn't looking. Clearly the scandal had hurt both the Culshaws deeply. But her grey eyes were warm and genuine, and Eve took to her immediately, the older woman wrapping her hands in her own. 'I'm so pleased you could come, Evelyn. Now, there's a name you don't hear terribly often these days, although I've met a few Eves in my time.'

'It was my grandmother's name,' she said, giving the other woman's hands a return squeeze, 'and a bit of a mouthful, I know. Either is perfectly fine.'

Maureen said something in return, but it was the movement in Eve's peripheral vision that caught her attention, and she glanced up in time to see something skate across Leo's eyes, a frown tugging at his brow, and for a moment she wondered what that was about, before Eric started introducing the Alvarezes, snagging her attention.

Richard Alvarez looked tan and fit, maybe fifteen years younger than Eric, with sandy hair and piercing blue eyes. His wife, Felicity, could have been a film star and was probably another ten years younger than he, dark where he was fair, exotic and vibrant, like a tropical flower in her gown of fuchsia silk atop strappy jewel-encrusted sandals.

Waiters unobtrusively brought platters of canapés and more glasses of champagne, topping up the others, and they settled into the lounge area, Leo somehow managing to steer them both onto the long sofa where he sat alongside her, clearly part of the act to show how close they were.

Extremely close apparently.

For he stretched back and looped an arm around her shoulders, totally at ease as he bounced the conversation between Eric and Richard, though

Eve recognised it for the calculated move it was. Yet still that insider knowledge didn't stop her catching her breath when his fingers lazily traced a trail down her shoulder and up again, a slow trail that had her senses humming and her nipples on high alert and a curling ribbon of desire twisting and unfurling inside her. A red ribbon. Velvet. Like the sound of Leo's voice…

'Evelyn?'

She blinked, realising she'd been asked a question that had completely failed to register through the fog of Leo's sensual onslaught. She captured his wandering fingers in hers, ostensibly a display of affection but very definitely a self-defence mechanism if she was going to be able to carry on any kind of conversation. 'Sorry, Maureen, you were asking about how we met?' She turned to Leo and smiled, giving his fingers a squeeze so he might get the message she could do without the manhandling. 'It's not exactly romantic. I'm actually his PA. I was handling all his paperwork and arrangements and suddenly one day it kind of happened.'

'That's right,' Leo added with his own smile,

fighting her self-defence measures by putting a proprietorial hand on her leg, smoothing down the silk of her gown towards her knee, bringing his hand back to her thigh, giving her a squeeze, setting up a sizzling, burning need. It was all Eve could do to keep smiling. She put her glass down and curled her fingers around the offending hand, squeezing her nails just a tiny bit too hard into his palm, just a tiny warning.

But he only looked at her and smiled some more. 'And this was after I'd sworn I'd never get involved in an office romance.'

Maureen clapped her hands together, totally oblivious of Eve's ongoing battle. 'Did you hear that, Eric? An office romance. Just like us!'

Eric beamed and raised his glass. 'Maureen was the best little secretary I ever had. Could type a hundred and twenty words a minute, answer the phone and take shorthand all at the same time. I could hardly let her go, could I?'

'Eric! You told me you fell in love with me at first sight.'

'It's true,' he said, with a rueful nod. 'Her first day in the job and the moment I walked in and saw the sexy minx sitting on her little swivel chair, I was toast. I just can't have that story getting around business circles, you understand.'

The men agreed unreservedly as Maureen blushed, her eyes a little glassy as she reached across and gave Eric's hand a squeeze. 'You're an old softie from way back, Eric Culshaw, and you know it.' She dabbed at her eyes with a lace handkerchief, and Eve, thinking she must look like she was shackled to Leo, shifted away, brushing his hand from her leg as she reached for her champagne. He must have got the message, because he didn't press the issue, simply reached for his own drink, and part of her wondered whether he thought he'd done enough.

Part of her hoped he did.

The other part already missed his touch.

'Felicity, how about you?' she said, trying to forget about that other wayward part of her. 'How did you and Richard meet?'

'Well...' The woman smiled and popped her glass on the table, slipping her hand into her husband's. 'This might sound familiar, but I'd been out with a friend, watching the sailing on

Sydney Harbour. It had been a long day, so we stopped off to have a drink in a little pub on the way home, and the next thing I know, this nice fellow came up and asked if he could buy us both a drink.' She turned to him and smiled and he leaned over and kissed her delicately on the tip of her nose. 'And the rest, as they say, is history.'

'That's just like Princess Mary and Prince Frederik of Denmark,' said Maureen. 'Don't you remember, everyone?' Eve did, but she never had a chance to say anything because Leo chose that precise moment to run his finger along the back of her neck, a feather-light touch that came with depth charges that detonated deep down inside her as his fingertips drew tiny circles on her back.

'It wasn't the same hotel, was it?' Maureen continued.

'No. But it's just as special to us. We go every year on the anniversary of that first meeting.'

'How special,' said Maureen. 'Oh, I do love Sydney and the harbour. I have to say, the warmer weather suits me better than Melbourne's, too.'

And Eve, lulled by the gentle touch of a master's hand, and thinking of her never-ending quest to get the washing dried and not looking forward to cold showers and boiling kettles so Sam could have a warm bath, couldn't help but agree. 'Sydney's wonderful. I used to work there. I spent so many weekends at the beach.'

The fingers at her neck stilled, a memory flickering like the frames of an old black and white movie in the recesses of his mind. Something about Sydney and a woman he'd met years ago so briefly—too briefly—*a woman called Eve.*

CHAPTER FIVE

WHAT was it Maureen had said? *'Most people would shorten it to Eve.'* And she'd said something like, *'Either is fine.'* The exchange had niggled at some part of him when he'd heard it, although he hadn't fully understood why at the time, but then the mention of Sydney had provided the missing link, and suddenly he'd realised that there could be no coincidence—that bit had provided the missing piece and the jigsaw had fitted together.

He thought back to a day that seemed so long ago, of flying into Sydney in the early morning, recalling memories of a whirlwind visit to rescue a deal threatening to go pear-shaped, and of a glass-walled office that had looked over Sydney Harbour and boasted plum views of both the Harbour Bridge and the Opera House. But the view had faded to insignificance when his eyes had happened upon the woman sitting in the opposite corner of the room. Her hair had been streaked with blonde and her skin had had a golden tan, like both had been kissed by the sun, and her amazing eyes had looked deeper and more inviting than any famous harbour.

And endless meetings and time differences and jet-lag had all combined to press upon him one undeniable certainty.

He'd wanted her.

'Eve,' she'd told him when he'd cornered her during a break and asked her name. Breathless Eve with the lush mouth and amazing eyes and a body made for sin, a body all too willing to sin, as he'd discovered in that storeroom.

And he'd cursed when he'd had to leave all too suddenly for Santiago, cursed that he'd missed out on peeling her clothes from her luscious body, piece by piece. He'd had half a mind to return to Sydney after his business in Chile concluded, but by then something else had come up. And then there'd been more business in other countries, and other women, and she'd slipped from his radar, to be loosely filed under the-ones-that-got-away.

It wasn't a big file and as it happened she hadn't got away after all. She'd been right there under his nose, answering his emails, handling his paperwork, organising meetings, and she'd never once let on. Never once mentioned the fact they'd already met.

What was that about?

His hand drifted back to his pretend fiancée's back, letting the conversation wash over him—something about an island the Culshaws owned in the Whitsundays—his fingertips busy tracing patterns on her satiny-soft skin as he studied her profile, the line of her jaw, the eyes he'd noticed and should have recognised. She was slightly changed, the colour of her hair more caramel now than the sun-streaked blonde it had been back then, and maybe she wasn't quite so reed thin. Slight changes, no more than that, and they looked good on her. But no wonder he'd thought she'd looked familiar.

She glanced briefly at him then, as the party rose and headed for the dining area, a slight frown marring an otherwise perfect brow, as if she was wondering why he'd been so quiet. He smiled, knowing that the waiting time to meeting her again had passed; knowing that her time had come.

Knowing that for him the long wait would soon be over. She'd been like quicksilver in his arms that day, so potent and powerful that he hadn't been able to wait the few hours before closing the deal to sample her.

There was no doubt in his mind that the long wait was going to be worth it.

So what, then, that he had a rule about not sleeping with his PA? Rules were made to be broken after all, some more than others. He smiled at her, taking her arm, already anticipating the evening ahead. A long evening filled with many delights, if he had anything to do with it. Which of course, he thought with a smile, he did.

Maybe it was the fact everyone so readily accepted Evelyn as his fiancée. Maybe it was the surprising realisation that playing the part of a fiancé wasn't as appalling or difficult as he'd first imagined that made the evening work.

Or maybe it was the thought of afterwards, when he would finally get the opportunity to peel off her gown and unleash the real woman beneath.

But the evening did work, and well. The drinks and canapés, the dinner, the coffee and dessert—the hotel catering would get a bonus. It was all faultless. Culshaw was beaming, his wife was glowing and the Alvarezes made such entertaining dinner companions, reeling out one amusing anecdote after another, that half the time everyone was laughing too much to eat.

And Evelyn—the delectable Evelyn—played her part to perfection. Though he frowned as he caught her glancing at her watch again. Perfect, apart from that annoying habit she had of checking the time every ten minutes. Why? It wasn't like she was going anywhere. Certainly not before they'd had a chance to catch up on old times.

Finally coffee and liqueurs had been served and the staff quietly vanished back into the kitchen. Culshaw stifled a yawn, apologising and blaming his habit of going for a long early walk every morning for not letting him stay up late. 'But I thank you all for coming. Richard and Leo, maybe we can get those contract terms nutted out tomorrow— what do you think?'

The men drew aside to agree on a time to meet while the women chatted, gathering up purses and wraps. They were nice people, Eve thought, wishing she could have met them in different circumstances, and not while living this lie. She knew she'd never meet them again, and maybe in the bigger scheme of things it made no difference to anything, as they would all go their separate ways in a day or so, but that thought was no compensation for knowing she'd spent the evening pretending to be someone and something she was not.

'Shall we go?' Leo said, breaking into her thoughts as he wrapped his big hand around hers and lifted it to his mouth, and Eve could see how pleased he was with himself and with the way things had gone.

The final act, she thought as his lips brushed her hand and his eyes simmered with barely contained desire. A look filled with heated promise, of a coming night filled with tangled limbs in tangled sheets. The look a man should give his fiancée before they retired to their room for the night. The final pretence.

No pretence necessary when her body responded like a woman's should respond to her lover's unspoken invitation, ripening and readying until she could feel the pulse of her blood beating out her need in that secret place between her thighs, achingly insistent, turning her thoughts to sex. No wonder everyone believed them to be lovers. He acted the part so very well. He made it so easy. He made her body want to believe it.

A shame, she thought as they said their final goodbyes and left the suite. Such a shame it was all for nothing. Such a waste of emotional energy and sizzling intensity. Already she could feel her body winding down, the sense of anticlimax rolling in. The sudden silence somehow magnified it, the hushed passage devoid of other guests, as empty as their pretend relationship.

'Will the car be waiting for me downstairs?' she asked, glancing at her phone as they waited in the lift lobby. No messages, she noticed with relief, dropping it back into her purse. Which meant Mrs Willis had had no problems with Sam.

'So anxious to get away?' the man at her side said. 'Do you have somewhere you're desperate to get to?'

'Not really. Just looking forward to getting home.' And she wasn't desperate. There no point rushing now, Eve knew. She'd been watching the time and chances were Mrs Willis was well and truly tucked up in bed by now, which meant no picking up Sam before morning. But equally there was nothing for her here. She'd done her job. It was time to drop the make-believe and go home to her real life.

'No? Only you kept checking your watch every five minutes through dinner and you just now checked your phone. I get the impression I'm keeping you from something—or someone.'

'No,' she insisted, cursing herself for being so obvious. She'd gone to the powder room to check her messages during the evening, not wanting to be rude or raise questions. She hadn't thought anyone would notice a quick glance at her watch.

'Look, it's nothing. But we've finished here, haven't we?'

'Aren't you forgetting something?'

'What?' He took her hand and lifted it, the sapphire flashing on her finger. 'Oh, of course. I almost forgot.' She tried to slip her hand from his so she could take it off, but he stilled her.

'Not here. Wait till we get to the suite.' And she would have argued that it wasn't necessary, that she could give it to him in the lift for that matter, only she heard voices behind them and the sound of the Alvarezes approaching and knew she had no choice, not when their suites were on the same floor and it would look bizarre if she didn't accompany Leo.

'Ah, we meet again,' Richard said, coming around the corner with Felicity on his arm as the lift doors whooshed open softly behind them. 'Great night, Leo, well done. Culshaw seems much more comfortable to do business now. He agreed to call to arrange things after his walk in the morning.'

Leo smiled and nodded. 'Excellent,' he said, pressing the button for the next floor as they made small talk about the dinner, within seconds the two couples bidding each other goodnight again and heading for their respective suites.

And, really, it wasn't a problem for Eve. Leo had told her his rule about not mixing business with pleasure. So she knew she had nothing to fear. She'd give him back the ring, make sure the coast was clear, and be gone. She'd be in and out in two minutes, tops.

He swiped a card through the reader, holding the door open so she could precede him into the room. She ignored the flush of sensation as she brushed past him, tried not to think about how good he smelt or analyse the individual ingredients that made up his signature scent, and had the ring off her finger and back in its tiny box before the door had closed behind her. 'Well, that's that, then,' she said brightly, snapping the box shut and setting it back on the coffee table. 'I think that concludes our business tonight. Maybe you could summon up that car for me and I'll get going.'

'You said you didn't have to rush off,' he said, busy extracting a cork from what looked suspiciously like a bottle of French champagne he'd just pulled from an ice bucket she was sure hadn't seen before, and felt her first shiver of apprehension.

'I don't remember that being there when we left.'

'I asked the wait staff to organise it,' he explained. 'I thought a celebration was in order.'

Another tremor. Another tiny inkling of… *what*? 'A celebration?'

'For pulling off tonight. For having everyone believe we were a couple. You had both Eric and Maureen, not to mention Richard and Felicity, eating out of your hand.'

'It was a nice evening,' she said warily, accepting a flute of the pale gold liquid, wishing he'd make a move to sit down, wishing he was anywhere in the suite but standing right there between her and the door. Knowing she could move away but that would only take her deeper into his suite. Knowing that was the last place she wanted to be. 'They're nice people.'

'It was a perfect evening. In fact, you make the perfect virtual fiancée, Evelyn Carmichael. Perhaps you should even put that on your CV.'

He touched his glass to hers and raised it. 'Here's to you, my virtual PA, my virtual fiancée. Here's to…us.'

She could barely breathe, barely think. There was no *us*. But he had that look again, the look he'd had before they'd left the presidential suite that had her pulse quickening and beating in dark, secret places. And suddenly there was that image back in her mind, of tangled bedlinen and twisted limbs, and a strange sense of dislocation from the world, as if someone had changed the rules when she wasn't looking and now black was white and up was down and nothing, especially not Leo Zamos, made any kind of sense.

She shook her head, had to look away for a moment to try to clear her own tangled thoughts.

'Oh, I don't think I'll be doing anything like this again.'

'Why not? When you're so clearly a natural at playing a part.' He nodded in the direction of her untouched glass. 'Wine not to your taste?'

She blinked and took a sip, wondering if he was ever going to move away from the minibar and from blocking the door, moving closer to the wall at her back in case he was waiting for her to move first. 'It's lovely, thank you. And the Culshaws and Alvarezes are lovely people. I still can't help but feel uncomfortable about deceiving them that way.'

'That's something I like about you, Evelyn.' He moved at last, but not to go past her. He moved closer, touching the pad of one finger to her brow, shifted back a stray tendril of hair, a touch so gentle and light but so heated and powerful that she shivered under its impact. 'That honest streak you have. That desire not to deceive. I have to admire that.'

Warning bells rang out in her mind. There was a calm, controlled anger rippling through the underbelly of his words that she was sure hadn't been there before, an iron fist beneath the velvet-gloved voice, and she wasn't sure what he thought he was celebrating but she did know she didn't want to be any part of it.

'I should be going,' she said, searching for the nearest horizontal surface on which to deposit her nearly untouched drink, finding it in the credenza at her side. 'It's late. Don't bother your driver. I'll get myself a cab.'

He smiled then, as lazily and smugly as a crocodile who knew that all the efforts of its prey were futile for there was no escape. a smile that made her shiver, all the way down.

'If you'll just move out the way,' she suggested, 'I'll go.'

'Let you go?' he questioned, retrieving her glass and holding it out to her. *When she was so clearly leaving.* 'When I thought you might like to share a drink with me.'

She ignored it. 'I had one, thanks.'

'No, that drink was a celebration. This one will be for old times' sake. What do you say, Evelyn? Or maybe you'd prefer if I called you *Eve.*'

And a tidal wave of fear crashed over her, cold and drenching and leaving her shuddering against the wall, thankful for its solidity in a world where the ground kept shifting. *He knew!* He knew and he was angry and there was no way he was going to move away from that door and let her calmly walk out of here. Her tongue found her lips, trying valiantly to moisten them, but her mouth was dry, her throat constricted. 'I'm good with either,' she said, trying for calm and serene and hearing her voice come out thready and desperate. 'And I really should be going.'

'Because I met an Eve once,' he continued, his voice rich and smooth by comparison, apparently oblivious to her discomfiture, or simply enjoying it too much to put an end to it, 'in an office over-looking Sydney Harbour. She had the most amazing blue eyes, a body built for sinful pleasures, and she was practically gagging for it. Come to think of it, she *was* gagging for it.'

'I was not!' she blurted, immediately regretting her outburst, wishing the shifting ground would crack open and swallow her whole, or that her pounding heart would break the door down so she could escape. Because she was kidding herself. Even if it hadn't been how she usually acted, even if it had been an aberration, he was right. Because if that person hadn't interrupted them in the midst of that frantic, heated encounter, she would have spread her legs for him right there and then, and what was that, if not gagging for it?

And afterwards she'd been taking minutes, writing notes, even if she'd found it nearly impossible to transcribe them or remember what had actually been said when she'd returned to her office because of thoughts of what had almost happened in that filing room and what would happen during the night ahead.

He curled his fingers under her chin, forced her to look at him, triumph glinting menacingly in his eyes. 'You've been working with me for more than two years, sweet little Miss Evelyn don't-like-to-deceive-anyone Carmichael. When exactly were you planning on telling me?'

She looked up at him, hoping to reason with him, hoping that reason made sense. 'There was nothing to tell.'

'Nothing? When you were so hot for me you were practically molten. And you didn't think I might be interested to know we'd more than just met before?'

'But nothing happened! Not really. It was purely a coincidence that I came to work for you. You wanted a virtual PA. You sent a query on my webpage. You agreed the terms and I did the work you wanted and what did or didn't happen between us one night in Sydney was irrelevant. It didn't matter.' She was babbling and she knew it, but she couldn't stop herself, tripping over the words in the rush to get them out. 'It wasn't like we ever had to meet. If you hadn't needed a pretend fiancée tonight, you would never have known.'

'Oh, I get it. So it's my fault, is it, that all this time you lied to me.'

'I never lied.'

'You lied by omission. You knew who I was, you knew what had so very nearly happened, and you failed to tell me that I knew you. You walked in here and hoped and prayed I wouldn't recognise you and you almost got away with it.'

'I didn't ask to come tonight!'

'No. And now I know why. Because you knew your dishonesty would come unstuck. All that talk about not deceiving people and you've happily been deceiving me for two years.'

'I do my job and I do it well!'

'Nobody said you didn't. What is an issue is that you should have told me.'

'And would you have contracted me if I had?'

'Who knows? Maybe if you had, we might be having great sex right now instead of arguing.'

Unfair, she thought as she sucked in air, finding it irritatingly laden with his testosterone-rich scent. So unfair to bring up sex right now, to remind her of what might have been, when she was right here in his suite and about to lose the backbone of her income because she'd neglected to tell him about a night when nothing had happened.

'Let me tell you something, Evelyn Carmichael,' he said, as he trailed lazy fingertips down the side of her face. 'Let me share something I might have shared with you, if you'd ever bothered to share the truth with me. Three years ago, I was aboard a flight to Santiago. I had a fifty-page report to read and digest and a strategy to close a deal to work out and I knew what I needed to be doing, but hour after hour into the flight I couldn't concentrate. And why couldn't I concentrate? Because my head was filled with thoughts of a blonde, long-limbed PA with the sexiest eyes I had ever seen and thinking about what we both should have been doing right then if I hadn't had to leave Sydney.'

'Oh.' It had never occurred to her that he might have regretted his sudden departure. It had never occurred to her that she hadn't been the only one unable to sleep that night, the only one who remembered.

'I felt cheated,' he said, his fingers skimming the line of her collarbone, 'because I had to leave before we got a chance to…get to know each other.' His fingers played at her shoulder, his thumbs stroking close to the place on her throat where she could feel her pulse beat at a frantic pace. 'Did you feel cheated, Evelyn?'

'Perhaps. Maybe just a little.'

'I was hoping maybe more than just a little.'

'Maybe,' she agreed, earning herself a smile in return.

'And now I find that I have been cheated in those years since. I never had a chance to revisit what we had lost that night, because you chose not to tell me.'

She blinked up at him, still reeling from the impact of his words. 'How could I tell you?'

'How could you not tell me, when you must know how good we will be together. We knew it that day. We recognised it. And we knew it earlier when I kissed you and you turned near incendiary in my arms. Do you know how hard that kiss was to break, Evelyn? Do you know what it took to let you go and take you to dinner and not take you straight to my bed?'

She shuddered at his words, knowing them to be true, knowing that if he'd taken her to bed that night, she would have gone and gone willingly. But he'd left her confused. He'd been angry with her a moment ago, yet now the air vibrated around them with a different tension. 'What do you want?'

'What I have always wanted ever since the first time I saw you,' he said, his eyes wild with desire and dark promises that kept those dark, secret places of her humming with sensation and aching with need. 'I want you.'

CHAPTER SIX

'THIS won't work,' she warned weakly, her hands reaching for the wall behind her as his mouth descended towards hers. 'This can't happen.'

He brushed her lips with his. 'Why not?'

'You don't sleep with your PAs. You don't mix business with pleasure. You said so yourself.'

'True,' he agreed, making a second pass over her mouth, and then a third, lingering just a fraction longer this time. 'Never mix business with pleasure.'

'Then what are you doing?' she asked, her senses buzzing. He slipped his hands behind her head, his fingers weaving through her hair as he angled her mouth higher.

'Unfinished business, on the other hand,' he murmured, his eyes on her mouth. 'That's a whole different rule book.' He moved his gaze until dark eyes met her own, gazing at her with such feverish intensity that she felt bewitched under their spell. 'Do you want to open that book, Evelyn? Do you want to dip into its pages and enjoy one night of pleasure, one night of sin, to make up for that night we were both cheated out of?'

This time he kissed her eyes, first one and then the other, butterfly kisses of heated breath and warm lips that made her tremble with both their tenderness and their devastating impact on her senses. 'Or do you still wish to leave?'

He kissed her lips then before she could respond, as if trying to convince her with his hot mouth instead of his words, and she could feel the tension underlining his movements, could tell he was barely controlling the passion that bubbled so close below the surface as he tried to be gentle with her. He was offering her a night of unimaginable pleasure, a night she'd thought about so many times since that ill-fated first meeting.

Or he was offering her escape.

She was so, so very tempted to stay, to stay with this man who'd invaded her dreams and longings, the man who'd taken possession of them ever since the day they'd first met. The man who had made her want and lust and feel alive for the first time in her life. She wanted to stay and feel alive again.

But she should go. The sensible thing would be to go. She was no longer a free agent, able to do as she pleased when she pleased. She had responsibilities. She was a mother now, with a child waiting at home.

His kisses tortured her with their sweetness while her mind grappled with the dilemma, throwing out arguments for and against. The decision was hers and yet she felt powerless to make it, knowing that whatever she decided, she would live to regret it.

But it was just one night.

And her child was safely tucked up in bed, asleep.

But hadn't her child resulted from just one such night? One foolish wrong decision and she would live with the consequences for ever. Did she really want to risk that happening again? Could she afford to?

Could she afford not to?

Did she really want to go home to her empty bed and know that she'd turned her back on this chance to stop wondering what if, the chance to finally burn this indecent obsession out of her system?

And didn't she deserve just one night? She'd worked hard to make a success of her business and to provide for Sam. Surely she deserved a few short hours of pleasure? Maybe then she could stop wondering, stop imagining what it would have been like to have made love that night, to have finished what they'd started. And maybe he was a lousy lover and this would cure her of him for ever, just like one night with Sam's father had been more than enough.

Hadn't she already paid the price?

His mouth played on hers, enticing her into the dance, his tongue a wicked invitation, his big hands skimming her sides so that his thumbs brushed the undersides of her breasts, so close to her aching nipples that she gasped, and felt herself pushing into his hands.

A lousy lover? *Not likely.*

'What's it to be?' he said, pulling back, his

breathing ragged, searching her eyes for her answer. 'Do I open the book? Or do you go? Because if you don't decide now, I promise you, there will be no going anywhere.'

And his words were so hungry, the pain of his restraint so clearly etched on his tightly drawn features, that she realised how much power she really held. He wanted her so much, and still he was prepared to let her walk away. Maybe because he sensed she was beyond leaving, maybe because he knew that his kisses and touches had lit a fire inside her that would not be put out, not be quenched until it had burned itself to ash. But he was giving her the choice.

When really, just like that first time, there was none.

'Maybe,' she ventured tentatively, her voice breathy as she wondered whether in wanting to make up for a lost opportunity she was making the mistake of her life, 'we could at least check out a page or two.'

He growled his approval, a sound straight from the Stone Age, a dark, deep sound that rumbled into her very bones and shook them loose. She would have fallen then, if he hadn't pulled her into his kiss, his hot mouth explosive on her lips, on her throat, as he celebrated her acquiescence, his arms like steel crushing her to him, his hands on her back, on her shoulders, capturing a breast and sweeping his thumb over her peaked nipple, sending sensation spearing down to that hot place between her thighs and making her mewl into his mouth.

'God, I want you,' he said, echoing the only words she was capable of thinking, as she pushed his jacket off his shoulders and he shucked off his shoes. He released her for only a moment, shrugged the jacket off and let it drop to the floor while she worked desperately at his buttons and his tie, and he turned his attentions to her zipper. She felt the slide down her spine and the loosening of fabric, the electric touch of his hands at the small of her back. Impatient to similarly feel his flesh under her hands, she ripped the last few buttons of his shirt apart, scattering them without regard.

Finally she had him, her hands on his firm chest, her fingers curling through the wiry thatch of hair, lingering over the hard, tight nubs of his nipples, relishing all the different textures of him, the hard and the hot, the wet and the insistent, and if she'd had any doubt at all that he wanted her, it was banished by the bucking welcome of that rigid column as her hand slid down to cup his length. He groaned and pushed her back hard against the wall as she grappled with his belt.

He was everywhere then, his taste in her mouth, his hands separating her from the dress, slipping the straps from her shoulders, letting it slip between them as he took her breasts, the scrap of lace no barrier against the heat from his hands. And then even that was gone, replaced by his hot mouth, devouring her, lapping and suckling at her flesh until she cried out with the agony and the ecstasy of it all. It was everything she had imagined in dreams spun in hot, torrid nights alone and more, and still it was not enough.

She clung to his shoulders as he laved her nipples, gathering her skirt as his hands skimmed up her legs, not taking his time but still taking so much longer than she wanted.

'Please,' she pleaded, clutching at his head,

gasping as he cupped her mound, his long fingers stroking her through panties wet for him, needing him, hot and hard, inside her. Needing him now, before she came with just one more touch. *'Please!'*

'God, you're so hot,' he said, dispensing with her underwear, pulling free his belt with damn near the same frenetic action.

She saw him then. Her first glimpse of him unleashed and hungry and pointing at her, a compass needle finding true north. Once she might have wanted to believe it. But she was wiser than to believe such fantasies these days, and much wiser to the consequences. Which reminded her…

'Protection,' she muttered through the fog of need, but he was already ripping open a sachet with his teeth, rolling it on before pulling her back into his kiss. Her breasts met his chest, the feel of skin against skin taking her breath away, or maybe it was what he was doing with his hands and clever fingers.

Her dress bunched at her waist, his hands kneading her behind, fingers teasingly close to the centre of her, driving her insane with need, as he lifted her, the wall at her back, still kissing her as he urged her legs around him until she felt him, thick and hard, nudging, testing, at her entrance.

She cried out, something unintelligible and primal, lost in an ocean of sensation, drowning under the depths. It was almost too much and yet it was nowhere near enough and she only knew that if she didn't get him inside her she would surely die of need.

He didn't keep her waiting. With a guttural cry of his own he lowered her, meeting her with his own thrust, until he was lodged deep inside her.

A moment in time. Just a moment, a fraction of a second perhaps, but Eve knew it for a moment about which she would always remember every single detail, the salt of his skin and the smell of his shampoo, the feel of his big hands paused at her hips, and the glorious feeling of the pulsing fullness inside her.

Could it get any better than this?

And then he moved, and it did, and flesh against flesh had never felt so good, every new moment giving her treasures to secrete away, to add to a store of memories she would take from this night, of sensations she would never forget. Sensations that built, one upon another, layer upon layer, higher and higher, fed by each calculated withdrawal, each powerful thrust.

Until there was no place to go, no place higher or brighter or more wondrous as the sensation, the friction, the furious rhythm of his pounding body all melded together into a cataclysm, taking her with it.

She screamed her release, throwing her head back against the wall, her muscles clamping down hard as he shuddered his own frenetic release.

She didn't know how long they stood together that way, she couldn't tell, too busy trying to replace the oxygen consumed in the fire of their coupling while her body hummed its way down from the peak. But slowly her feet found the floor, slowly her senses and sensibility returned. To the knowledge she was standing barely dressed between a wall and a near naked man she barely knew but with whom she'd just had mind-blowing sex.

'Wow,' she said, embarrassed in the aftermath as he dispensed with the condom and she remembered her own wantonness. Had she really pulled his shirt apart in her desperation to get inside it? Had she really cried out like a banshee?

And he laughed, a low rumble in a velvet coat. 'Evelyn Carmichael,' he told her with a chaste kiss to her lips, 'you are just one surprise package after another.'

He didn't know the half of it. She found the straps of her dress, pulling it up to cover herself before she started looking for her underwear.

'Leave it,' he said, his hand around her wrist. 'There's no point. It's only coming off again.'

'Again?'

His eyes glinted. 'This book I was telling you about. It's a long book,' he said. 'That was only chapter one.'

She blinked up at him, her dress gathered in front of her, and he pulled her arm away, letting the dress drop to her waist, then slide over her hips in a whisper of silk to pool like a lake on the floor.

And even though they'd just had sex, she felt nervous standing there before him wearing nothing more than lace-topped stockings and spiky sandals. She hadn't been with anyone since Sam's father. She didn't have the body she'd once had, her belly neat but traced with tiny silvery lines and softer than it had been before bearing a child.

She held her breath. Could he tell? Would it matter?

'You look,' he said, 'like a goddess emerging from the sea.' And some tiny, futile creature somewhere deep inside her grew wings and attempted a fluttery take-off.

'And you look like a pirate,' she countered, reminding herself it was just a game. It wasn't real and that pointless tiny creature inside her would soon die a rapid death, its gossamer wings stilled. 'Ruthless and swashbuckling.'

'Uncanny,' he said, his lips turning in a half-smile as he swung her into his arms. 'However did you know?'

'Know what?' she asked, feeling a secret thrill as he carried her into the next room.

'The goddess of the sea and the swashbuckling pirate.' He winked at her and he laid her gently on the king-sized bed. 'That's the title of chapter two.'

It was a long and detailed chapter. There were passages Eve found agonising going, like when the pirate sampled the goddess, tasting every last inch of her except *there*, where she craved his detailed attentions the most, and then there were the passages that moved at what felt like breakneck speed, where he feasted on her until she was bucking on the bed.

And even when she lay, still gasping, after her latest orgasm, the chapter didn't end and he joined her in savouring the final few pages together until that final breathtaking climax.

Outside the lights of Melbourne winked at her, the skies unusually clear, a heavy full moon hanging above the bridge over the Yarra.

Inside the suite, Eve's breathing slowly returned to normal as she savoured the feel of Leo's arm lying proprietorially over her stomach as he lay face down alongside her, his eyes closed, his lips slightly parted, his thick black hair mussed into bed-head perfection by her own hands. He wasn't asleep, she knew, but it was a wonder given the energy he'd used tonight. Definitely a pirate, she thought. And very definitely a magic night. But it was late and magic nights had to end, just as goddesses had responsibilities too.

Oh, my, he'd actually called her a goddess! And she felt that tiny winged creature launch itself for another lurching spin around her stomach.

'I should go,' she said, with a wistful sigh for the ill-fated beast before she returned to sensible Evelyn Carmichael again and considered the practicalities of not having a functioning hot water service. 'Do you mind if I take a shower before I go?'

And his eyes blinked open, the arm around her waist shifting, scooping higher to capture a breast. A smile played on his lips while he coaxed a nipple into unexpected responsiveness. 'I've got a much better idea.'

She swallowed. Surely it wasn't possible? But

still her body hummed into life at the thought. 'Chapter three?'

He nodded, his busy fingers hard at work on the other nipple, adding his hot mouth to the mix, guaranteeing the result. 'The goddess returns to the sea only to find the pirate lurking in the depths, waiting to ambush her.'

'That's a long title.'

'It's a long chapter,' he said, rolling off the bed and scooping her up into his arms. 'In which case, we should get started.'

An hour later Eve had bubbles up to her chin and warm jets massaging all those newly found muscles of hers she hadn't realised would so appreciate the attention. From the bedroom came the sound of Leo's voice on the phone as he arranged her car. In a moment she'd have to prise herself from the bath and shower off the bubbles but for the moment she lingered, her limbs heavy, feeling languorous and spoilt and thoroughly, thoroughly spent.

It was easy to feel spoilt here, she thought, quietly reflecting on her opulent surroundings, committing them to memory as part of the experience. For if the size and scale of the suites had amazed her, the sheer lavishness of the bathroom had taken her breath away.

Marble in muted tones of sun-ripened wheat and golden honey lined the floor and walls, the lighting low and warm and inviting, the spa and shower enclosure—a space as big as her entire bathroom at home—separated from the long marble vanity by heavy glass doors. It was utterly, utterly decadent.

And if there hadn't been enough bubbles, he'd found champagne and ripe, red strawberries to go with it. He'd turned what she'd intended simply as a shower into another erotic fantasy.

What a night. Three chapters of his book, all of them different, every one of them a complete fantasy. If chapter one had been desperate and frenetic, and chapter two slow to the point of torture, chapter three had showed the pirate at his most playfully erotic best. The slip of oils on skin, the play of the jets on naked flesh and the sheer fun of discovering what lay beneath the foam.

She closed her eyes, allowing herself just a few

snatched seconds of imagining what it would be like if this was her life, all posh hotels with views of city lights and an attentive lover like Leo to make her feel the most special woman alive, with no worries about broken-down appliances and falling-down houses.

But then there was Sam.

And she felt guilty for even thinking of a world that didn't include him—that couldn't include him. For Sam was her life, whereas this was a fantasy that had no other course but to end and end soon.

She slipped under the water one last time, letting her hair fan out around her head, relishing the big wide bath, before she sat up, the water sluicing from her body. No regrets, she told herself as she squeezed the water from her hair, she wouldn't allow it. She'd made her choice. She would live with it. And whatever happened in her life after this, whatever her everyday suburban life might hold, she knew she would have this one secret night of passion to look back on.

'The car will be waiting in half an hour,' Leo said, returning to the bathroom, a white towel slung perilously low over his hips, and even though she knew what lay beneath, even though she knew what that line of dark hair leading down from his navel led so tantalisingly and inexorably to, she couldn't look away. *Or maybe because of it.* 'Will that give you enough time for that shower you wanted and get dressed?'

And even though she knew this moment was coming, Eve still felt a pang, the fabric of her fantasy starting to unravel, as already she started counting down the minutes. Just thirty of them to go before she turned from one-night lover to a billionaire into long-term single mother. But there was nothing else for it. She nodded. 'Plenty of time,' she said.

He offered her his hand rather than the towel she would have preferred and she hesitated, before realising that after the things they'd done together this night, there was no point in being coy. So she rose, taking his hand to prevent her slipping as she stepped out, and taking half the foam with her. Something about the way his body stilled alerted her. She was taller than him now, standing in the raised bath like this, and his eyes drank her in. 'What is it?' she said, looking down to see patches of foam sliding down her body and clinging to her breasts, the pink nub of one nipple peeping through. And she looked back to him to see him shaking his head, his dark eyes hot and heavy with desire. 'Suddenly I'm not so sure it will be anywhere near enough time.'

Something sizzled in her veins, even while her mind said no. 'You can't be serious.'

He gave a wry smile as he reached out to brush the offending nipple with the pad of one finger, sending tremors through her sensitive flesh, and he smoothed away more of the suds to reveal patches of skin, piece by agonising piece. 'It's still early.'

'Leo,' she said, ignoring the pleas her body was making to stay right where she was and stepping out to snap on the shower taps before she could take his words seriously. A torrent rained down from the cloudburst showerhead and she stepped into it, determined to be rid of the bubbles regardless of the water temperature. 'It's three o'clock in the morning. I'm going home.'

He peeled the towel from his hips, turned on his own shower. 'We have all night.'

'No. I have to go.' She turned her face away from the sight of his thickening member and up into the stream of water, relishing the drenching. It was cooler than she would normally prefer, but it was helping to clear her mind, helping cool her body down. And very definitely she needed to cool down. What kind of man could make love so many times in one night and still come back for more? When had fantasy ever collided so perfectly with reality? Well, that was apart from the reality she would no doubt be exhausted tomorrow while Sam would be his usual bundle of energy. *Today*, she reminded herself. He'd be up in a few short hours. She really needed to get home if she was to get any sleep tonight. 'Besides, you have an important deal to close.'

'So maybe I can give you a call, pick you up after-wards?'

Her heart skipped a beat and she paused, soap in hand, feeling only the pounding of the cascading water, the thudding of her heart and the flutter of those damned tiny wings. Without turning around, she said, 'I thought you were planning on leaving for London the minute you concluded the Culshaw deal.'

His mouth found her shoulder, his arms wrapping around her belly, and there was no missing that growing part of him pressing against her back, no missing the rush of blood to tissues already tender. And even though she knew his words meant nothing, nothing more anyway than him wanting a repeat performance in bed, it was impossible not to lean her head back against his shoulder just one last sweet time. 'I don't think that would be wise.' She turned off the water and peeled herself away, reaching for a towel as she exited the shower. 'We both agreed this was just one night. And while it's been good, I think, given our working relationship, that it's better left that way.'

'Only good?' he demanded, and she rolled her eyes. Trust the man to home in on the least important detail of the conversation. He followed her from the stall, swiping his own towel from the rack and lashing it around his hips, not bothering to wipe the beads of water from his skin so that his chest hair formed scrolls like an ancient tattoo down his chest to his belly and below.

Oh, my…

She squeezed her eyes shut. Grabbed another towel and covered her head with it, rubbing her hair frantically so she couldn't see him, even if she opened her eyes. 'All right. The sex was great. Fabulous.'

The towel blinding her eyes was no defence against the electric touch of his fingers at her shoulders. 'Then why shouldn't we meet again? It's not as if I'm asking for some long-term commitment.'

That's just it, she yearned to say. There's no future in it. There's nothing but great sex and the longer that happens, the greater the risk that I start to believe it's about more than that, and I can't afford to let that happen.

Not when she had Sam…

One night of sin was one thing. But she could not contemplate any kind of affair. What Sam needed was stability, not his mother embarking on a series of meaningless one-night stands, passing him off to whoever could look after him. She shook her head, heading for the bedroom, her clothes and a return to sanity. 'I can't sleep with you and work with you at the same time.'

'So become my mistress instead of my PA.'

She blinked, blindsided once again by the night's increasingly insane developments, pulling on her underwear in a rush, slipping off the towel to fix her bra, needing the shelter of her dress.

'Are you kidding?'

'You're right,' he said, without a hint of irony. 'Who could I get to replace you? So why can't you be both?'

'Perfect.' She slipped into her dress, retrieved her stockings and sat on the end of the bed, hastily rolling them up her legs. 'I thought you'd never ask. And when you get sick of me being your mistress, you can get me to send myself one of those trinkets you're so fond of sending to your ex-playmates. I already know where to send it. How efficient would that be?'

'Evelyn?'

She was busy in her purse, searching for a

comb in order to slick back and twist up her wet hair and not finding one. 'What?'

'Anyone might think you were jealous.'

'Jealous? Me?' She scooted past him back into the bathroom. Pulled a comb from the complimentary supplies boxed up on the vanity, raking it through her hair before twisting it up and securing it with a clip. It was rough but it would do until she got home. She certainly wasn't going to hang around here, styling her hair or trying to reapply make-up that would just have to come off at home anyway. 'Jealous of what?'

He leaned an arm up against the door, muscles pulling tight under his skin, making the most of the posture, and she cursed the fact he hadn't thought to put on anything more than a towel yet. Or maybe that was his intention. To remind her what she'd be missing out on. Well, tough. After tonight she knew what she'd be missing out on. Of course, he was tempting, but there came a time where self-preservation came first.

'You did make a point about having to send out those gifts to…my friends.'

'Your ex-lovers, you mean.'

'You *are* jealous.'

She shrugged. 'No. I've had my one night with you. Why should I be jealous?'

'Well, something's bugging you. What is it?'

She turned toward him then, wishing she could just walk away, sensitive to the fact that she could still be at risk of losing her contract if she angered him but still bothered enough by the riddle that was Leo Zamos to ask. 'You really want to know?'

'Tell me.'

'Okay,' she started, her eyes taking this last opportunity to drink in the glorious definition of his body, wanting to imprint all she could upon her memory before she left, because after tonight her memories would be all she had. 'What I don't understand is you.'

He laughed, a rich, deep sound she discovered she liked too much. 'What's so hard to understand?'

'Everything. You're confident and successful and ultra-rich—you have your own plane, for heaven's sake!—and you're a passionate lover and clearly have no trouble finding women willing to share your bed...' She paused for a moment, wondering if she'd said enough, wondering if she added that he was drop-dead gorgeous and had a body that turned a woman's thoughts to carnal acts, she would be saying more about herself than about him.

He smiled. 'That's it? I'm not actually sure where your problem lies.'

'No, that's not it. You know there's more. People are drawn to you, Leo, you know it. And it's just that, with everything you have going for you, I don't understand how it can be that when you feel the need to play happy families, you have to pay someone to pretend to be your fiancée.'

'You would have done it for free?' He gave a wry smile. 'I'll remember that for next time.'

'No!' she said, knowing she was making a hash of it, knowing he was laughing at her. 'That's not my point at all. I just don't understand why you're in the situation where you need to pretend. How is it that a man with clearly such great appeal to women hasn't got a wife or a fiancée or even a serious girlfriend? How is that possible?'

The smile slipped as he pushed away from the

wall, moving closer, the menacing glint in his eyes putting her on sudden alert. 'Maybe,' he said, drawing near, touching his fingers to her brow, tracing a line south, 'it's because there is no lack of women willing to share my bed. What is that delightful saying? Why buy a book when you can join a library?'

She stood stock-still, resisting the tremors set off by his merest touch, hating the smug look on his face, forcing a smile to hers. 'Well, the loan on this particular book just expired. Goodnight, Leo.'

He let her go, at least as far as the door.

'Evelyn.'

She halted, put her hand on the doorframe to stop herself swaying, and without turning around said, 'Yes?'

'Something I tell all the women I spend time with. Something I thought you might have understood, although, given your questions, maybe you need to hear it too.'

She looked over her shoulder, curious about what it was he told his 'women', what he thought she needed to hear. 'Yes?'

'I like women. I like sex. But that's where it starts and finishes. Because I don't do family. It's not going to happen.'

This time she took a step towards him, stunned by his sheer arrogance. 'You think I was on some kind of fishing expedition to work out what my chances were of becoming Mrs Leo Zamos for real?'

'You were the one asking the questions.'

'And I also said I don't want to see you again. Which part of "I don't want to see you again" equates to "Please marry me" exactly?'

'I was just saying—'

'And I'm saying you needn't have bothered. I'm not in the market for a husband as it happens, but even if I were, I'm certain I'd prefer someone who didn't profess to liking women and sex quite so much!' She turned on her heel and strode through the bedroom, slipping on her heels and picking up her purse, scanning the room for anything she might have left.

'Evelyn!'

But she didn't stop until she was through the living room then, turned, one more question to be answered before she left. 'I'll understand if you no longer want to retain me as your PA.'

'Don't be ridiculous. Of course I want to keep you.'

She nodded, relieved, suddenly realising how perilously close she'd come to blowing things. 'All right. All the best with the deal tomorrow. I guess I'll be hearing from you in due course.' She offered him her hand, back to brisk, businesslike efficiency, even if she was dealing with a man wearing nothing more than a towel. 'Thank you for a pleasant evening, Mr Zamos. I'll see myself out, under the circumstances.'

One eyebrow quirked at the formality but he took her hand, squeezing it gently. 'It was my pleasure, Evelyn. My pleasure entirely.'

Minutes later, she sank her head back against the plush leather headrest and sighed as the limousine slipped smoothly from the hotel. Better to end this way, she reflected; better that they had argued rather than agreeing to meet again. Better that it had ended now when anything else would merely have been putting off the inevitable.

For it would have ended, nothing surer, and

probably as soon as their next meeting. And then Leo would take off in his jet and find another convenient Evelyn somewhere else in the world, and she would be forgotten.

But now they'd claimed their stolen night, the night they'd been cheated out of by conspiring circumstances those years ago, and it had been an amazing night and she'd managed to survive with both some degree of pride and her job intact. But it was for the best that it had ended on a sour note.

Now they could both put it behind them.

CHAPTER SEVEN

SHE grappled with the front-door key, her baby growing heavier by the minute. That or her night of sinful and unfamiliar pleasures had taken it out of her, but the child dozing on her shoulder felt like he'd doubled in size and weight overnight. Then again, maybe he'd just had one too many pancakes. She knew she had. She'd woken this morning after too few hours' sleep almost ravenous.

She was barely inside the door when the phone started ringing and she picked it up more to shut it up than any desire to talk to whoever was calling. She had less desire to talk when she found out who it was.

'Evelyn, it's Leo.'

The sound of his voice sent ripples of pleasure through her, triggering memories formed all too recently to not remember every single sensual detail. She sucked in air, but Leo was the last person she'd expected to call and there was nothing she could think of to say. Hadn't they said everything that needed to be said last night?

'Evelyn?'

She squeezed her eyes shut, trying to ignore the snatches of memory flashing through her mind, the rumble of his murmured words against her thigh, the brush of his whiskered cheek against her skin, his clever tongue…

'I…I didn't expect to hear from you.'

'I didn't expect to be calling. Look, Evelyn, there's been a development. Culshaw wants to move the contract discussions to somewhere where the weather suits Maureen better. He suggested we reconvene on his island off North Queensland.'

With the dead-to-the-world weight of her toddler on her shoulder, she battled to work out what it was Leo actually wanted. 'So you need me to make some bookings? Or do I have to rearrange your schedule?'

'Neither.' A pause. 'I need you to come.'

Sam stirred on her shoulder, his head lolling

from one side to the other, and she kissed his head to soothe him. 'Leo, you know that's not possible.'

'Why isn't it possible?'

'You said our deal was for one night only and I already told you I wouldn't meet you again.'

'But that was before Culshaw came up with this idea.'

'That's too bad. I did what we agreed.' And then, thinking he might better understand it in business-speak, 'I fulfilled the terms of the contract, Leo, and then some.'

'So we make a new deal. How much this time, Evelyn?' he asked, sounding angry now.

'I told you before, it's not about the money.'

'Fifty thousand.'

'No. I told you, they're nice people. I don't want to lie to them any more.'

'One hundred thousand.'

She looked up at the ceiling, cursing under her breath, trying not to think about what a sum like that would mean to the timing of her renovation plans. She could engage a decent architect, get quotes, maybe landscaping so Sam had a decent play area outside. But it was impossible. 'No!'

'Then you won't come?'

'Absolutely not.'

'So what am I supposed to tell Culshaw?'

'It's your lie, Leo. Tell him what you like. Tell him it's family reasons, tell him I'm sick, tell him I never was and never will be your fiancée. It's your call.' On her shoulder her son grew unsettled, picking up on the vibe in the air, butting his head from side to side against her shoulder, starting to grizzle.

'What was that?' Leo demanded.

'Me about to hang up. Are we finished here? Only it's not really a convenient time to call.' Please, God, can we be finished here? she prayed as her muscles burned under Sam's weight.

'No. I need...I need some documents to take with me!'

'Fine,' she said, sighing, wondering which documents they could possibly be when she was sure she'd provided him with everything he needed already and in triplicate. 'Let me know which ones and I'll email them straight away.'

'No. I need them in hard copy. All originals. You have to bring them to the hotel, as soon as you can.'

If she'd had a free hand, it would have gone to her head. 'I've always emailed documents to you before. It's never been a problem.'

'I need those documents delivered to me personally this afternoon!'

She sucked in a breath. 'Okay. I'll get them couriered over as soon as I can.'

'No. Definitely not couriered. You need to deliver them personally.'

'Why?'

'Because I need them immediately and they're commercial-in-confidence. I'm not about to entrust them to someone else, not at this crucial stage. You'll have to bring them yourself.'

When she made no response, she heard, 'You did say you wanted to keep working with me.'

Bastard! She could take a veiled threat just as well as she could take a hint. She was damned if she'd take more of Leo's money to pretend to be his fiancée, but right now she couldn't afford to ditch him as a client. 'Of course. I'll bring them over myself.'

'Good. I'll be in my suite.'

'Not there.'

'What?'

'I won't bring them to your suite. I won't go there again. Not after...'

'You think I'd try something?'

Hardly, after the way they'd parted last night. But she didn't trust herself not to be tempted, there in that room where they'd done so many things... How could she be in that room and see that wall and know how it felt to have her back to it and have him between her legs and driving into her? How could she calmly pretend nothing had happened? How could she not want it to happen again?

She swallowed, trying not to think of all the reasons she didn't want to be in that room. 'I just don't think it would be wise.'

She heard his rushed expulsion of air. 'Okay,' he said. 'Let's play it your way. Culshaw's taking Maureen out to visit friends so we should be safe to meet in the bar. I'll buy you a coffee—is that permissible?'

She nodded into the phone, relieved at least they'd be meeting somewhere public. Sam settled back on her shoulder. 'A coffee would be fine.'

He clicked off his phone, cursing softly. So she wouldn't come to the room. But she had agreed to come. Of course she could have emailed the documents, but then he'd have no way of convincing her to come to the island with him. He could convince her, he had no doubt. Look at how she had all but melted in his arms last night with just one kiss! And once she was back in his bed, she'd get over whatever hang-up she had about coming with him. He was already looking forward to it.

Because while sex was easy to come by, great sex wasn't, and last night had definitely registered right up there with the best. And while he'd been content for it to end last night the way it had—it would have ended some time anyway— the opportunity to have her in his bed for another couple of nights held considerable appeal.

He could do much worse than sharing his bed with Evelyn.

He'd soon make it happen. Once she was here, he'd just have to come up with a way to get her up to his suite and convince her how much she wanted to come with him. He'd think of something.

His phone rang, a glance at the caller ID assuring him it wasn't Evelyn calling back to change her mind about meeting him.

'Eric,' he said, relieved, his mind already working on a plan to get Evelyn up to his suite. 'What can I do for you?'

But relief died a quick death as Culshaw explained how Maureen was looking to book a day in the island resort's spa for the women and wanted to know if Evelyn might be interested. Leo knew he had to say something now, in case she refused to change her mind.

'Look, Eric, about Evelyn, you might want to warn Maureen. It seems there's a slight chance she might not be able to make it after all...'

'I wish I could help, lovey,' Mrs Willis said, when Evelyn nipped over to ask if she would mind babysitting again, this time only for an hour or so, 'but my brother Jack's just had an episode and I promised to go and help Nancy with him. He gets terribly confused, poor love. I was going to pop by and tell you, because I might be away for a few days.' She stopped folding clothes for a moment, her creased brow folding along time worn lines. 'I hate leaving you, though, with the hot water not working and no family to help out. Such a tragedy to lose your parents so young and then your granddad. They've all missed out on so much, watching you grow up and now Sam.' She shook her head. 'Such a pity.'

'I know,' Eve said softly, feeling a pang of sadness for her grandfather and for parents she could barely remember. 'But don't worry. You do too much for me as it is. We'll be fine. I'll call Emily down the street. She's always on the lookout for some extra cash.'

Except when she called it was to hear Emily was already working a shift at the local supermarket. Which left Evelyn with only one option.

Not such a bad option, she reflected as she turned onto the freeway and pointed her little city commuter towards the city, wondering why it hadn't occurred to her earlier. She hadn't wanted to tell Leo about her child, figuring it was none of his business and that it might prejudice his opinion of her as someone able to handle his workload, but neither did she trust him not to try to change her mind by fair means or foul. And then there was the matter of not trusting her own wayward desires. Look where they'd landed her last night—right in Leo Zamos's bed. Not to mention his spa bath…

She shivered, unable to suppress either a secret smile or the delicious shimmy at the memories of his mouth seeking her breasts as he raised her over him, of his hungry mouth at her nipples as he probed her entrance, of the long, hard length of him filling her as he pulled her down on him inch by glorious inch, a shimmy that radiated out from muscles tender and sore and clearly still far too ready to party.

Oh, no, there was no way she could trust herself with him.

And if there was one certain way to ensure that there would be no repeats of last night's performance, it was to take her child along. Leo didn't do family, and clearly didn't want one. He'd made that abundantly clear and she was grateful he had. For it had put paid to that tiny creature that insisted on fluttering around inside her despite what she'd known in her head all along to be true. That his interest in her began and finished with sex. There could be no future with him. There was no future for them.

And with just one look at Sam he'd forget all about wanting to play make-believe with her. One look at Sam and he'd never want to see her again. Which suited her just fine.

It was foolproof!

Forty minutes later the doorman helped her unload both her baby stroller and a sleeping Sam startled into wakefulness from the car. She settled him, watching his eyelids flutter closed again, still sleepy from the journey, lowering the back and tucking his favourite bear by his side so he would feel secure and snooze on as long as possible. Soon enough he'd be demanding to get out and explore this new world—she just prayed he'd last until she got him out of the hotel. Not that the meeting should take longer than ten minutes when it was only documents she had to hand over. Probably less, she thought with a smile, doubting Leo would stick around long enough for coffee when he saw what else she'd brought with her.

She could hardly wait to see his face.

The subtly lit lounge wasn't busy, only a few tables occupied this time of the day, couples sharing coffee and secrets, family groups gathered around tables enjoying afternoon tea.

She found a hotel phone, asked Reception to let Mr Zamos know she was there, and stopped a while in awe to admire, over the balcony, the amazing sweeping stairway that rose grandly from entry level and the water feature that spilled and spouted between levels of the hotel. She must commit this to memory, she thought. It was the place of fairy-tales, of princes and princesses, and not of the real world, and of ordinary people like her who had blown hot water services and frazzled appliances to replace.

She settled into a booth that offered some degree of privacy, gently rocking the stroller.

Sam wasn't buying it, jerking into wakefulness, this time taking in the unfamiliar surroundings with wide, suspicious eyes.

'It's okay, Sam,' she said, reaching for the stash of food she'd brought and had tucked away in the baby bag. 'We're visiting, that's all. And then I'll take you for a walk along Southbank. You'll like that. There's a river and lots of music and birds. Maybe we might even spot you a fish.'

'Fith!' He grinned, recognising the word as she handed him his favourite board book and he reached for a sultana with the other. 'Fith!'

He'd been waiting on the call, all the while working out a strategy that would get her out of the lounge and up into his room. At last he'd hit on the perfect plan, so simple it couldn't fail. He'd play it cool, accept the documents she'd brought without mention of the trip away and without trying to change her mind, and see her to her car, remembering once they'd got to the lifts something he'd meant to bring down for her—it wouldn't take a moment to collect it from his suite…

He hit the second floor with a spring in his step. Oh, he loved it when a plan came together.

He scanned the lounge for her, skipping over the groups and couples, searching for a single woman sitting no doubt nervously by herself. Had she been able to forget about last night's love-making yet? He doubted it. Even though the night had ended on a sour note, those flashbacks had kept him awake thinking about it half the night. When Culshaw had mooted this idea of going away for the weekend, he'd initially been appalled. It was bad enough that the closing of the deal had been held up by last night's dinner, without having to endure still more delays while Culshaw soothed his wife's wounded soul with an impromptu holiday. Until he'd worked out that he could easily endure a couple of more nights like the last. Very easily.

And then he saw her sitting with her back to him in a little booth off to one side, her hair twisted high behind her head, making the most of that smooth column of neck. Just the sight of that bare patch of skin sent such a jolt of pure lust surging through him, such a heady burst of memories of her spread naked on his sheets, that it was hard to think over the pounding of the blood in his veins, other than to want to drag her to his room and prove why she needed to come with him until she begged him not to leave her behind.

In another time, maybe even in another part of this world, he would do exactly that, and nobody would stop him, nobody would think twice.

But there was more reason than the mores of the so-called civilised world that stilled his savage urges. For he knew what he might become if he let the animal inside him off the leash.

Never had he felt so close to that beast. Why now? What was it about her that gave rise to such thoughts? She was the means to an end, that was why he needed her. Nothing more. Great sex was just a bonus.

She turned her head to the side then, her lips moving as if she was talking to someone, but there was nobody there, nothing but a dark shape in the shadowed recess behind the sofa, a dark shape that had him wondering if he'd found the wrong woman the closer he got. Because it made no sense…

She looked around at the exact time his brain had finally come to terms with what his eyes were telling him, at the precise moment the cold wave of shock crashed over him, washing away his well-laid plans and leaving them a tangled and broken mess at his feet.

'Hello, Leo,' she said, closing the picture book she was holding in her hands. 'I've brought those documents you asked for.'

She'd brought a hell of a lot more than documents! In the dark shape he'd worked out was a pram sat a baby—a child—holding onto the rail in front of him and staring wide-eyed and open-mouthed up at Leo like he was some kind of monster. It didn't matter that the kid was probably right. He looked back at Evelyn. 'What the hell is this?'

'Leo, meet my son, Sam.' She turned toward the pram. 'Sam, this is Mr Zamos. If you're very nice, he might let you call him Leo.'

'No!' Sam pushed back in his stroller and twisted his body away, clearly unimpressed as he pushed his face under his bear and began to grizzle.

'I'm sorry,' she said, one hand reaching out to rub him on the back. 'He's just woken up. Don't worry about coffee, it's probably better I take him for a walk.' She picked up a folder from the table and stood, holding it out for Leo. 'Here's all the documents you asked for and I've flagged where signatures are required. Let me know if there's anything else you need. I promised Sam a walk along the river while we're here, but we'll be home in a couple of hours.'

He couldn't say anything. He could barely move his hand far enough to accept the folder she proffered. All he could think of was that she had a child and she hadn't told him. What else hadn't she told him? 'You said there wasn't a Mr Carmichael.'

'There's isn't.'

'Then whose is it?'

'His name is Sam, Leo.'

'And his father's name?'

'Is none of your business.'

'And is that what you told him when he asked you where you were all night?'

She shook her head, her eyes tinged with sadness. 'Sam's father doesn't figure in this.'

His eyes darted between mother and child, noticing for the first time the child's dark hair and eyes, the olive tinge to the skin, and he half wondered if she was bluffing and had borrowed someone else's baby as some kind of human shield. He would have called her on it but for noticing the angle of the child's wide mouth and the dark eyes stamped with one hundred per cent Evelyn, and that made him no happier.

Because someone else had slept with her.

He thought of her in his arms, her long-limbed body interwoven with his, he thought of her eyes when she came apart with him inside her, damn near shorting his brain. And now he thought of her coming apart in someone else's arms…

'You should have told me.'

'Why?'

'Damn it, Evelyn! You know why!'

'Because we spent the night together?' she

hissed. Sam yowled, as if he'd been on the receiving end of that, and she leaned over, surprising Leo when she didn't smack him, as he'd half expected, but instead delicately stroked the child's cheek and calmed him with whispered words. Something twisted inside him, something shapeless and long buried, and he had to look away lest the shape take form and he worked out what it was. His gut roiled. What was happening to him? Why did she have this effect on him? She made him feel too much. She made him see too much.

She made him remember things he didn't want to remember.

And none of it made sense. None of it he could understand.

'I'm sorry you feel aggrieved,' she said, and reluctantly he turned back to see her unclipping the child's harness and lifting the child into her arms, where he snuggled close, sniffling against her shoulder as she rubbed his back. 'But what part of our contract did I miss that said I should stipulate whether I should have children or what number of them I should have?'

'Children? You mean there's more?'

She huffed and turned away, rubbing the boy's back, whispering sweet words, stroking away his hiccups, and the gentle sway of her hips setting her skirt to a gently seductive hula.

'Ironic isn't it?' she threw at him over her shoulder. 'Here you are, so desperate to prove to Eric Culshaw that you're some kind of rock-solid family man, and you're scared stiff of a tiny child.'

'I'm not—'

She spun around. 'You're terrified! And you're taking it like some kind of personal affront. But I wouldn't worry. Sam's a bit old for anyone to believe he was conceived last night, so there's no reason to fear any kind of paternity claim.'

'You wouldn't dare!'

'Oh, you do flatter yourself. A woman would have to be certifiably insane to want to shackle themselves to you!'

'Clearly Sam's father was of the same mind about you.'

He knew he'd hurt her. He recognised the precise moment when his words pierced the fighting sheen over her eyes and left them bewildered and wounded. He almost felt regret. Almost wanted to reach out and touch her cheek like she'd touched her child's, and soothe away her pain.

Almost.

But that would mean he cared. And he couldn't care about anyone. Not that way.

And just as quickly as it had gone down, the armour was resurrected and her eyes blazed fire at him. 'I have a child, Mr Zamos. It's never affected the quality of my work to date and it's my intention that it never will, but if you can't live with that then fine, maybe it's time we terminated our agreement now and you found someone else to look after your needs.'

Bile, bitter and portentous, rose in the back of his throat. She was right. There was no point noticing her eyes or the sensual sway of her hips. There was no point reliving the evening they'd had last night. She couldn't help him now and it was the now he had to be concerned with. As to the future, maybe it was better he found someone else. Maybe someone older this time. It wasn't politically correct to ask for a date of birth, but he'd never been any kind of fan of political correctness. Especially not when it messed with his plans. He huffed an agreement. 'If that's what you want.'

She stood there, the child plastered against her from shoulder to hip, his arms wound tightly around his mother's neck, the mother so fierce he was reminded of an animal fighting to protect its litter that he'd seen on one of those television documentaries that appeared when you were flicking through the channels on long-haul flights. The comparison surprised him. Was that how all mothers were supposed to be?

'In that case,' she said, 'I'll burn everything of yours onto disk and delete it from my computer. I'll send it to you care of the hotel. You can let them know your forwarding address.'

His hands clenched at his sides, his nails biting into his palms. 'Fine.'

'Goodbye, Mr Zamos.' She held out her hand. 'I hope you find whatever it is you're looking for.' Her words washed over him, making no sense as he looked down at her hand. The last time he would touch her. The last time they would meet skin to skin.

How had things gone so wrong?

He wrapped his hand around hers, her hand cool against his heated flesh, and he felt the tremor move through her, saw her eyelids flutter closed, and despite the fact she represented everything he didn't want in this world, everything he hated and despised and had promised himself he would never have, still some strange untapped part of him mourned her loss.

Maybe that was how it started, though, with this strange want, this strange need to possess.

Maybe it was better to let her go now, he thought, while he still could. While she was still beautiful.

But still it hurt like hell.

Unable to stop himself, unable to let her go just yet, his other hand joined the first, capturing her hand, raising it to his mouth for one final kiss.

'Goodbye Evelyn,' he said, his voice gravel rich, tasting her on his lips, knowing he would never forget the taste of her or the one night of passion they'd shared in Melbourne.

'Leo! Evelyn!' came a voice from over near the bar. 'There you are!'

CHAPTER EIGHT

EVE gasped, tugging to free her hand, the fight-or-flight instinct telling her to get out while she still could, but Leo wasn't about to let her go, his grip tightening until she felt her hand was encased in steel. 'This is your fault.' He leaned over and whispered in her ear as Eric Culshaw bounded towards them, beaming from ear to ear. 'Remember that.' And then he straightened and even managed to turn on a smile, although his eyes were anything but relaxed. She could almost hear the brain spinning behind them.

'Eric,' Leo said, his velvet voice all charm on the surface, springloaded with tension beneath. 'What a surprise. I thought you were taking Maureen out.'

He grunted. 'She spotted some article in a woman's magazine—you know the sort of thing—and grew herself a headache.' He shook his head.

'Sordid bloody affair. You'd think the reporters could find something else to amuse themselves with by now.' And then he huffed and smiled. 'Which makes you two a sight for sore eyes.' His eyes fell on the dozing child in her arms. 'Although maybe I should make that three. Who's this little tacker, then?'

Almost as if aware he was being discussed, Sam stirred and swung his head round, blinking open big dark eyes to check out this latest stranger.

'This is Sam,' Eve said, her tongue feeling too big for her mouth as she searched for things she could tell him that wouldn't add to the lie tally. 'He's just turned eighteen months.'

Culshaw grinned at the child and Sam gave a wary smile in return before burying his head back in his mother's shoulder, which made the older man laugh and reach out a hand to ruffle his hair. 'Good-looking boy. I thought you two were playing things a bit close to the chest last night. When were you going to tell us?'

Eve felt the ground lurch once more beneath her feet. Eric thought Sam was *theirs*? But, then, of course he would. They were supposed to have been a couple for more than two years and Sam's father was of Italian descent. It would be easy to mistake Sam's dark eyes and hair for Leo's. Why would they question it?

But she couldn't let them keep thinking it. Weren't there enough lies between them already?

'Actually,' she started, 'Sam—'

Her efforts earned her a blazing look from Leo. 'Eve doesn't like to give too much away,' he said, smiling at Eric, glancing back in her direction with a look of cold, hard challenge.

Suddenly Maureen was there too, looking pale and strained, her mood lifting when she saw Sam, clucking over him like he was a grandchild rather than the child of someone she'd only just met.

'You didn't tell us you had such an adorable little boy,' she admonished, already engaging Sam in a game of peek-a-boo before holding out her hands to take him.

'Some people wouldn't approve,' Eve offered stiffly, ignoring Leo's warning glare as she handed Sam over, then adding because of it, 'I mean, given the fact we're not married and all.'

'Nonsense,' Eric said, pinching Sam's cheek. 'There's no need to rush things, not these days.'

Leo smiled, his eyes glinting triumphantly as Maureen settled into a chair and jogged Sam up and down on her knees, making him chuckle.

'So,' said Eric, following his wife's lead and pulling up a chair, and soon demanding equal time with Sam, 'I assume Sam explains the "family reasons" you weren't going to be able to join us on the island?'

Eve dropped into a chair, feeling like she was being sucked deeper and deeper into a web of deceit. Leo must have warned them she might not be coming and used one of the excuses she'd suggested.

'That was my fault, Eric,' he said coolly. 'I figured that a toddler was hardly conducive to contract deliberations.'

'He can be very disruptive,' she added. 'Especially when he's out of his routine. You wouldn't believe what a handful he can be.'

'What, this little champion?' Bouncing the laughing toddler on his knee with such delight until it was impossible to work out who was laughing the most, Eric or Sam, as the toddler got the horsy ride of his life. 'You must come,' he said, slowing down to take a breather.

'More,' demanded Sam, bouncing up and down. 'More!'

Culshaw laughed and obliged, though at a much gentler pace. 'You will come, won't you? After all, it's hardly fair to keep you two apart when you barely get to see each other as it is. You will love it, I promise. Tropical island paradise. Your own bungalow right on the beach. We'll organise a cot for Sam and a babysitter to give you a real break. I imagine you don't get too many of those, working for Leo and looking after this little chap. How does that sound?'

Eve tried to smile, not sure she'd succeeded when the ground beneath her felt so unsteady. 'It does sound lovely.' And it did. A few days on a tropical island paradise with nothing more to do than swim or read or sip drinks with tiny umbrellas. The bungalow probably even had hot running water. Except she'd be sharing that bungalow with *him*. 'It's just that—'

'Oh, please,' Maureen added, putting her hand

on Eve's arm. 'Last night was the best time I've had for ages. I know it's asking a terrible lot of everyone and disrupting everyone's schedules, but right now it would mean so very much to me.'

'Of course they'll come,' she heard Leo say, 'won't you, Eve?'

And finally the unsteady ground she'd felt shifting under her feet the last few days opened up and swallowed her whole.

A smiling flight attendant greeted them, cooing over Sam, as Eve carried him on her hip into the jet. Eve just nodded in return, weariness combining with a simmering resentment. As far as she was concerned, this was no pleasure trip and she certainly wasn't happy about how she'd been manipulated into coming.

And then she stepped into the plane and found even more reason to resent the man behind her. It looked more like a luxury lounge room than any plane interior she'd ever seen before, the cabin filled not with the usual rows and rows of narrow seats and plastic fittings and overhead lockers but a few scattered wide leather armchairs with timber cabinet work trimmed with bronze. Beyond the lounge area a door led to what must be more rooms and Eve caught a glimpse of a dining table with half a dozen chairs in a recessed alcove.

So much wealth. So much to impress. Leo Zamos seemed to have everything.

Everything but a heart.

Maybe that's how you got to be a billionaire, she mused as another attendant showed her to a pair of seats where someone had already fitted her child restraint to buckle Sam in more securely. She helped settle the pair in and to stow their things, chattering pleasantly all the time while Eve stewed as she stashed books and toys close by and missed every word.

It all made sense. No wonder Leo Zamos was the success he was. Being ruthless in business, ruthless in the bedroom, taking what you wanted when you wanted—a heart would surely get in your way if you had one.

And while Eve simmered, Sam, on the other hand, was having the time of his tiny life, relishing the adventure and the attention, his dark eyes filled with glee as he pumped his arms up and down and made a sound like a war cry.

'I think someone approves,' Leo said from the seat alongside when the attendants had gone to fetch pre-flight drinks.

'His name is Sam,' she hissed, her resentment bubbling over at how she'd been trapped into this weekend away, a weekend of continued pretence with people who didn't deserve to be lied to. The only bright spots she could see were that the Culshaws and the Alvarezes were travelling together on the Culshaws' jet, and that they would all have private quarters, which meant she didn't have to pretend being madly in love with Leo twenty-four seven. She couldn't have stood the strain of it all if she had. As it was, she didn't know now how she was going to keep up the charade.

The attendant brought their drinks, advised there were two minutes until departure and discreetly disappeared.

What a mess. Eve poured a box of juice into a two-handled cup and passed it to a waiting Sam, along with a picture book to occupy him for a few minutes. How was she expected to act like Leo's loving fiancée now? It had been so much easier last night when there had been so much sexual tension and simmering heat sparking between them. Now the tension and the heat had more to do with anger.

All to do with anger, she corrected herself with a sigh. She was over him, even if he did have a velvet voice and the body of a god.

Across the aisle, the subject of her dark thoughts raised his drink. 'You sound like you have a problem.'

'Funny you should mention that.'

'You could have said no.'

'I did say no, remember? And then you turned around and said yes, of course we would come!'

He shrugged, as if it didn't matter, and if they'd been on any normal kind of plane, Eve could have given in to the desire to smack him. 'What can I say? Maureen likes you. It means the world to her that you can go.'

'You don't care about Maureen,' she said, keeping her voice low so she didn't alarm Sam. 'You don't care about anyone. All you care about is yourself and what you want, and you'll do anything to keep this deal from going off the rails, even if it means lying to people.'

'You don't know anything.'

'I know you made the right decision to never get married. Because I understand you now, and I understand what makes you tick, and you might have a fortune and a private jet and do okay in the sack with women, but you have a stone where your heart should be.'

His dark eyes glinted coldly, his jaw could have been chiseled from the same hard stone from which his heart was carved. 'Thank you for that observation. Perhaps I might make my own? You seem very tense, Evelyn. I think you might benefit from a couple of days relaxing on a tropical island.'

Bastard! Eve turned away, checking on Sam as the cabin attendant collected their glasses and checked all was ready for take-off.

The jet engines wound up as the plane taxied to the runway and Sam looked up in wonder at her, excited but looking for reassurance at the new sounds and sensations. She stroked his head.

'We're going on a plane, Sam. We're going on a holiday.'

And Sam squealed with delight and the plane raced down the runway and lifted off. *Good on you, Sam,* Eve thought, finding the book she'd hoped to read a few pages of as the plane speared into the sky, *at least one of us might as well enjoy the weekend.*

She must have dozed off. Bleary eyed, she found her book neatly placed by her side, while beside her Sam was grizzling softly but insistently, unable to settle.

'What's wrong?' Leo asked, putting aside the laptop he was working on as she unbuckled Sam from his seat and brought him against her chest.

'It's his nap time. He might settle better on my lap.' She searched for the chair's controls, although it was hard to manoevre with Sam's weight on her chest. 'Does this seat recline?'

'I've got a better idea. There's still a couple of hours' flight time to go. You might both be more comfortable in the bedroom. Let me show you the way.'

And the idea of a real bed in which to cuddle

up and snooze with Sam sounded so wonderful right now, she didn't hesitate.

Maybe if she hadn't been so bone-weary. Maybe in an ordinary airline seat, by holding onto the back of the seat in front of her to pull herself up, she could have managed it. Then again, she realised, maybe if she'd thought to undo her seat belt she could have done it. Damn.

'What is it?' he said, when she didn't follow him.

'Can you take Sam for a moment? My seat belt's still done up.'

Leo turned into a statue right before her eyes, rigid and unblinking as he stared down at her restless child. And if she wasn't mistaken, that look she saw in his eyes was fear.

'Take him?'

'Yes,' she said, her hands under his arms, ready to hand him over. 'Just for a second. I just need to undo my seat belt.'

'I...'

'I'll give you a hand,' said one of the cabin attendants, slipping past the stunned Leo.

'I've been secretly hoping for a cuddle of this gorgeous boy.'

She took Sam from her and swung him around, jogging him on her hip so that he stopped grizzling, instead blinking up at her with his big dark eyes, plump lips parted. 'You are gorgeous, aren't you? You're going to be a real heartbreaker, I can tell.' And then to Eve, 'How about I carry him for you? I'm probably more used to the motion of the plane.' Eve smiled her thanks, retrieving Sam's bear from the seat as Leo remembered how to move and led the way.

'There you go,' the attendant said a few moments later, as she peeled back the covers and laid the drowsy child down. 'Press this button,' she said, pointing to a console on the side table, 'if there's anything else I can help you with.' And with a brisk smile to them both and one last lingering look at Sam, she was gone.

'Thank you for thinking of this,' Evelyn said, sitting down alongside her son and tucking his bear under his arm. And then, because she felt bad about the things she'd said to him earlier and without taking her eyes from Sam, she said, 'I'm sorry for what I said earlier. I had no right.'

'Forget it,' he said, his velvet voice thick with gravel. 'For the record, you were probably right. Now, there's an en suite through that door,' he continued, and she looked over her shoulder, surprised to see a door set so cleverly into the panelling that she'd missed it as she'd looked around.

'Oh, I thought that was the bathroom we passed on the way. Next to the galley.'

'That serves the other suite.'

'Wow,' Eve said, taking it all in—the wide bed, the dark polished timber panelling and gilt-edged mirror and adding it to what she'd already seen, the dining table and spacious lounge. 'Incredible. A person could just about live in one of these things, couldn't they?'

'I do.'

Her head swung back. 'When you're travelling, you mean?'

'You know my diary, Evelyn. I'm always travelling. I live either in the plane or in some hotel somewhere.'

'So where's home?'

He held out his arms. 'This is home. Wherever I am is home.'

'But you can't live on a plane. Everyone has a home. You must have family somewhere.' She frowned, thinking about his voice and the lack of any discernable accent. Clearly he had Mediterranean roots but his voice gave nothing away. 'Where do you come from?'

Something bleak skated across his eyes as he looked at his watch. 'You're obviously tired and I'm keeping you both. Have a good sleep.'

He turned to leave then, turned back, reaching into his pocket. 'Oh, you'd better have this back.' He set the tiny box on the bedside table. Eve blinked at it, already knowing what it held.

'They extended the loan?'

He gave a wry smile. 'Not exactly. But it's yours to keep afterwards.'

'You bought it?'

'It looks good on you. It matches your eyes.'

She looked from the box to the man, still stroking her son's back, aware of his soft breathing as he settled into a more comfortable sleep. Thank heavens for the reality of Sam or she could easily think she was dreaming. 'What is this?' she said, mistrustful, the smouldering sparks of their earlier confrontation glowing brightly, fanned by this latest development. 'Some kind of bribe so I behave properly all weekend?'

'Do I need it to be?'

'No. I'm here, aren't I? And so I'm hardly likely to make a scene and reveal myself as some kind of fraud. But I'm certainly not doing it for your benefit, just like I'm not doing it for any financial gain. I just don't want to let Maureen down. She's had enough people do that recently, without me adding to their number.'

'Suit yourself,' he said, his voice sounding desolate and empty. 'But if you change your mind, feel free to consider it your parting trinket. And just like you said, you won't even need to post it to yourself. So efficient.'

And then he was gone, leaving only the sting of his parting words in his wake. She kicked off her shoes and crawled into the welcoming bed, sliding her arm under Sam's head and pulling him in close. She kissed his head, drinking deeply of his scent and his warm breath in an attempt to blot out the woody spice of another's signature tones.

She was so confused, so tired. Sleep, she told herself, knowing that after a late night of sexual excesses followed by today's tension, what she really needed was to sleep. But something tugged at her consciousness and refused to let go as his words whirled and eddied in her mind, keeping her from the sleep she craved so much as she tried to make sense of what Leo had said.

A heart of stone she'd accused him of, and when she'd apologised, he'd told her she was probably right. She shivered just thinking how forlorn he'd looked. How lost.

A man with a stone for a heart. A man with no home.

A man with everything and yet with nothing.

And a picture flashed in her mind—the photographic print she'd seen in Leo's suite before dinner last night.

She'd been looking for a distraction at the time, looking for something to pretend interest in if only so she didn't have to look at him, so her eyes would not betray how strongly she was drawn to him. Only she hadn't had to feign interest when she'd seen it, a picture from the 1950s, a picture of a riverbank and a curving row of trees and a park bench set between.

Something about the arrangement or the atmosphere of that black and white photograph had jagged in her memory at the time, just as it struck a chord now. It was the old man sitting all alone on that park bench, hunched and self-contained, and sitting all alone, staring out over the river.

A lonely man.

A man with no family and nowhere to call home.

A man with nothing.

And it struck her then. Twenty or thirty years from now, that man could very well be Leo.

It was just a hiccup, Leo told himself as he considered the task ahead, just a slight hitch in his plans. Only a weekend, three nights at most, and the deal would be wrapped up once and for all. After all, Culshaw knew that even though they all called the shots in their respective businesses, none of them could just drop everything and disappear off the face of the earth—not for too long anyway. Neither could he risk them walking away. It had to be tied up this weekend.

He sighed as he packed up his laptop. He'd got precious little done, not that he'd expected to, with a child running riot. Only this one he'd barely seen and still he'd got nothing done.

Maybe because he couldn't stop thinking about her.

What was it about the woman that needled him so much? She was so passionate and wild in bed, like a tigress waiting to be unleashed, waiting for him to let her off the chain. Wasn't that enough? Why couldn't she just leave it at that? Why did she have to needle him and needle him and lever lids off things that had been welded shut for a reason? All her pointless questions. All working away under his skin. And why did she even care?

Two days. Three nights. So maybe extending his time in her presence wasn't his preferred option, but he could survive being around Evelyn that long, surely. After all, he'd had mistresses who'd lasted a month or two before he'd lost interest or moved cities. Seriously, what could possibly happen in just a weekend?

Hopefully more great sex. A sound sleep would do wonders to improve her mood, and a tropical island sunset would soon have her feeling romantic and back in his arms. Nothing surer.

And in a few short days he'd have the deal tied up and Evelyn and child safely delivered home again.

Easy.

'Mr Zamos,' the cabin attendant said, refreshing his water, 'the captain said to tell you we'll be landing in half an hour. Would you like me to let Ms Carmichael know?'

He looked at his watch, rubbed his brow, calculating how long she'd slept. If his theory was right, her mood should be very much improved already. 'Thank you,' he said, 'but I'll do it.'

There was no answer to his soft knock, so he turned the handle, cracked open the door. 'Evelyn?'

Light slanted into the darkened room and as his eyes adjusted he could make her out in the bed, her caramel hair tumbling over the pillow, her face turned away, her arm protectively resting over her child's belly.

Mother and child.

And he felt such a surge of feeling inside him, such a tangle of twisted emotions, that for a moment the noise of that blast blotted everything else out, and there was nothing else for it but to close his eyes and endure the rush of pain and disgust and anger as it ripped through him.

And when he could breathe again, he opened his eyes to see another pair of dark eyes blinking up at him from the bed. Across the sleeping woman, the pair considered each other, Leo totally ill equipped to deal with the situation. In the end it was Sam who took the initiative. He pulled his teddy from his arms and offered him to Leo. 'Bear.'

He looked blankly at the child and immediately Sam rolled over, taking his toy with him, then promptly rolled back and held his bear out to Leo again. 'Bear.'

And Leo felt—he didn't know how he felt. He didn't know what was expected of him. He was still reeling from the explosion of emotions that had rocked through him to know how to react to this.

'Bear!'

'Mmm, what's that, Sam?' Eve said drowsily, and she looked around and saw Leo. 'Oh.' She pushed herself up, ran a hand over her hair. 'Have I overslept?'

Her cheek was red where it had lain against the pillow, her hair was mussed and there was a smudge of mascara under one eye, but yet none of that detracted from her fundamental beauty. And he felt an insane surge of masculine pride that he was the one responsible for her exhaustion. And a not-so-insane surge of lust in anticipation of a repeat performance in his near future.

'We'll be landing soon. You don't want to miss the view as we come in. It's pretty spectacular, they tell me.'

It *was* spectacular, Eve discovered after she'd freshened herelf up and changed Sam before joining Leo back in the cabin. The sea was the most amazing blue, and she could make out in the distance some of the islands that made up the Whitsunday group. From here they looked like jewels in the sea, all lush green slopes and white sand surrounded by water containing every shade of blue. The sun was starting to go down, blazing fire, washing everything in a golden hue.

'That's Hamilton Island,' he said, indicating a larger island as they circled the group for their approach. 'That's where we'll land before transferring to the helicopter for Mina Island.'

'It's beautiful,' she said, pointing over Sam's shoulder. 'Look, Sam, that's where we're going for a holiday.' Sam burst into song and pumped his arms up and down.

It did look idyllic, she thought. Maybe a couple of days relaxing on a tropical island wouldn't be such a hardship. She glanced over at the man beside her, felt the familiar sizzle in her veins she now associated with him and only him, and knew she was fooling herself.

With Leo around things were bound to get complicated. They always did.

Which meant she just had to establish a few ground rules first.

CHAPTER NINE

'I'M NOT sleeping with you.'

They'd landed on Hamilton Island and made the helicopter transfer to Mina without incident, arriving to be greeted by Eric just as the sun was dipping into the water in a glorious blaze of gold. Eric had laughed, secretly delighted she could tell, when they'd all stood and watched the spectacle, telling them they'd soon get used to 'that old thing', before dropping them off at their beachside bure to freshen up before dinner.

And now, after a tour of the timber and glass five-star bungalow, their eyes met over the king-sized bed. The *only* bed, aside from the cot set up for Sam in the generous adjoining dressing room.

She wasn't about to change her mind. 'You'll just have to find yourself somewhere else to sleep.'

'Come on, Evelyn,' he said, sitting down on the bed and slipping off his shoes, peeling off his socks, 'don't you think you're being just a little melodramatic? It's not like we haven't slept together before.'

'That was different.'

He looked over his shoulder at her, one eyebrow raised. 'Was it?'

Her arms flapped uselessly at her sides. From outside she could hear Sam laughing as Hannah, the young woman who had been sent to be his babysitter, fed him his dinner. At least that part of the arrangements seemed to be going well.

'I'm not sharing a bed with you,' she said. 'And I certainly don't have to sleep with you just because we happen to be caught in the same lie.'

He stood, reefing his shirt from his pants as he started undoing the buttons at his cuffs. 'No? Even though you know we're good together?'

She blinked. 'What are you doing?'

He shrugged. 'Taking a shower before dinner,' he said innocently enough, although she saw the gleam in his eyes. 'Care to join me?'

'No!'

But she couldn't resist watching his hands moving over the buttons, feeling for them, pushing them through the holes. Clever hands. Long-fingered hands. And as he tweaked the buttons she was reminded of the clever way he'd tweaked her nipples and worked other magic... She looked away. Looked back again. 'There's no point. No point to any of it.'

'It's only sex,' he said, finishing off the rest of the buttons before peeling off his shirt. 'It's not like we haven't already done it—several times. And I know for a fact you enjoyed it. I really don't know why you're making out like it's some kind of ordeal.'

'It was supposed to be for just one night,' she said, trying and failing not to be distracted by his broad chest and that line of dark hair heading south. 'A one-night stand. No strings attached.'

'So we make it a four-night stand. And I sure as hell don't see any strings.'

She dragged her recalcitrant eyes north again, wondering how he could so easily consider making love to a person like they had for not one but four nights, and not want to feel some kind of affection for the other party. But, then, he had a head start on her. He had a heart of stone. 'It was nice, sure. But that doesn't mean we have to have any repeat performances.'

'There's that word again.' His hands dropped to the waistband of his pants, stilled there. '"Nice". Tell me, if you scream like that for nice, what do you do for mind-blowing? Shatter windows?'

She felt heat flood her face, totally mortified at being reminded of her other wanton self, especially now when she was trying to make like she could live without such sex. 'Okay, so it was better than nice. So what? It's not as if we even like each other.'

'And that matters because…?'

She spun away, reduced to feeling like some random object rather than a woman with feelings and needs of her own, and crossed to the wall of windows that looked out through palm trees to the bay beyond. It was moonlit now, the moon dusting the swaying palm leaves with silver and laying a silvery trail across the water to the shore, where tiny waves rippled in, luminescent as they kissed the beach. It was beautiful, the air balmy and still, and she wished she could enjoy it. But right now she was having trouble getting past the knowledge that she'd spent an entire night, had bared herself, body and soul, to a man who treated sex as some kind of birthright.

And if it wasn't bad enough that he'd not so subtly pointed out she'd been vocally enthusiastic, now he'd as much as agreed that he didn't even like her. Lovely.

And that was supposed to make her happier about sleeping with him?

Fat chance.

She felt his hands land on her shoulders, his long fingers stroking her arms, felt his warm breath fan her hair. 'You are a beautiful woman, Evelyn. You are beautiful and sexy and built for unspeakable pleasure. And you know it. So why do you deny yourself that which you so clearly desire?'

Self-preservation, she thought, as his velvet-coated words warmed her in places she didn't want warmed and stroked an ego that wanted to be liked and maybe, maybe even more than that.

'I can't,' she said. *Not without losing myself*

in a place I don't want to be. Not without risking falling in love with a man who has no heart.
'Please, just believe me, I'll pretend to be your fiancée, I'll pretend to be your lover. But, please, don't expect me to sleep with you.'

The big house, as the Culshaws referred to it, was exactly that. Not flashy, but all spacious tropical elegance, the architecture, like that of the bures, styled to bring the outside in with lots of timber and glass and sliding walls. Outside, on an expansive deck overlooking the bay and the islands silhouetted against the sky, a table had been beautifully laid, but it was the night sky that captured everyone's attention.

'I don't think I've ever seen so many stars,' Eve confessed, dazzled by the display as they sat down for the meal. 'It's just magical.'

Eric laughed. 'We think so. This island takes its name from one of them but don't ask me to point out which one.'

Maureen continued, 'When we first came here for a holiday about thirty years ago, we got home to Melbourne and wanted to turn right back round again. We've been coming here every year since. Hasn't been used much lately, not since—'

Eric cut in, saving her from finishing. 'Well, it's good to have guests here again, that's for sure. So I'd like to propose a toast. To guests and good friends and good times,' he said, and they all raised their glasses for the toast.

'Now,' Eric said, from alongside Leo, 'how's that young man of yours settling in?'

'He's in his element,' Eve replied. 'Two of his favourite things are fish and boats. He can't believe his good fortune.'

'Excellent. And the babysitter's to your satisfaction? Did she tell you she's hoping to study child care next year?'

'Hannah seems wonderful, thank you.'

Maureen distracted her on the other side, patting her on the hand. 'Oh, that reminds me, I've booked the spa,' she started.

But Eve didn't hear the rest, not when she heard Eric ask Leo, 'How old did you say Sam was again?'

She froze, her focus on the man beside her and how he replied to the question, the man stumbling with an answer, seemingly unable to remember the age of his own supposed child.

'Ah, remind me again, Eve?' he said at last. 'Is Sam two yet?' Eve excused herself and smiled, forcing a laugh.

'You go away much too much if you think Sam's already had his birthday. He's eighteen months old. How could you possibly forget?'

Leo snorted and said, 'I never remember this milestone stuff. It's lucky Evelyn does,' which earned agreement from Eric at least.

'It must be hard on you, though, Evelyn, with Leo always on the move,' Maureen said. Eve wanted to hug the woman for moving the conversation along, although a moment later she wished she'd opted for a complete change of topic. 'Do you have family nearby who help out?'

She smiled softly, looking up at the stars for just a moment, wondering where they were amidst the vast array. Her grandfather had held her hand and taken her outside on starry nights when she hadn't been able to stop crying and had told her they were up there somewhere, shining brightly, keeping her grandmother company. And now her grandfather was there too. She blinked. 'I have a wonderful neighbour who helps out. My parents died when I was ten and—I hate to admit it—I don't remember terribly much about them. I lived with my grandfather after that.'

'Oh-h-h,' said Felicity. 'They never got to meet Sam.'

'No, and I know they would have loved him.' She took a breath. 'Oh, I'm sorry for sounding so maudlin on such a beautiful night. Maybe we should change the topic, talk about something more cheerful.'

'I know,' said Eric jovially. 'So when's the happy day, you two?'

Eve wanted to groan, until she felt Leo's arm around her shoulders and met his dazzling smile. 'Just as soon as I can convince her she can't live without me a moment longer.'

Somehow they made it through the rest of the evening without further embarrassment but it was still a relief to get back to their bure. The long day had taken its toll, the stress of constantly fearing they would be caught out weighing heavily on Eve, and even though she'd slept on the plane, she couldn't wait to crawl into bed. *Her bed*, because after their earlier discussion, Leo had offered to sleep on the sofa. Hannah was sitting on it now, watching music television on low. She stood and clicked the remote off as they came in.

'How was Sam?' Eve asked, looking critically at the sofa, frowning at its length. Or lack of it. How the hell did Leo think he was going to fit on that?

'Sam's brilliant. I let him stay up half an hour longer, like you suggested, and he went down easy as. I checked him the last time about five minutes ago, and he hadn't stirred. I don't think I've ever looked after such a good baby.'

Eve smiled, relieved. 'Lucky you didn't meet him last week when he was teething—you might have had a different opinion.' She opened her purse to find some notes and Hannah waved her away. 'No. It's all taken care of. It's my job to look after Sam while you're here.' She headed for the door, gave a cheery wave. 'I'll see you in the morning, then.'

Eve met Leo coming out of the bedroom with an armful of pillows and linen. 'Goodnight,' he said, heading for the sofa maybe a little too stoically.

She watched him drop it all on the sofa, measured the height and breadth of man against length and width of sofa and realised it was never going to work. It should be her sleeping on the sofa. Except Sam's room was beyond the bedroom and it would be foolhardy if not impossible to move him now.

She watched him for a while try to make sense of the bedding, as if he was ever going to be comfortable there.

And suddenly she was too tired to care. It wasn't like they were strangers after all. They had made love and several times. And even if they didn't like each other, surely they could share two sides of a big wide bed and still manage to get a good night's sleep?

'Stop it,' she said, as Leo attempted to punch his pillow into submission at one end, one bare foot sticking out over the other. 'This is ridiculous.'

'You don't say.'

'Look, it's a big bed,' she said reluctantly, gnawing her lip, trying not to think of the broad, fit body that would be taking up at least half of it. 'We can share it.' Then she added, 'So long as that's all we share. Is that a deal?'

He sat up on a sigh, clearly relieved. 'It's a promise. I promise not to share anything, so long as you don't jump me first.'

'Ha. And I thought you were awake. Now I know you're dreaming. I'm going to have a shower—alone. You'd better be in bed and asleep when I get there, or it's straight back to the sofa for you.'

And he was asleep when she slipped under the covers, or he was good at pretending. She clung close to her edge of the bed, thinking that was the safest place, yet she could still feel the heat emanating from his body, could hear his slow, steady breathing, and tried not to think about what they'd been doing twenty-four hours ago, but found it hard to think of anything else. Especially when she was so acutely aware of every tiny rustle of sheets or shift in his breathing.

Twenty-four hours. How could so much have

happened in that time? How could so much change?

Outside the breeze stirred the leaves in the trees, set the palm fronds rustling, and if she listened hard, she could just hear a faint swoosh as the tiny swell rushed up the shore. But it was so hard to hear anything, so very hard, over the tremulous beating of her heart…

It was happening again. He buried his head under the blanket and put his hands over his ears but it didn't stop the shouting, or the sound of the blows, or the screams that followed. He cowered under the covers, whimpering, trying not to make too much noise in case he was heard and dragged out too, already dreading what he'd find in the morning at breakfast. If they all made it to breakfast.

There was a crash of furniture, a scream and something smashed, and the blows continued unabated, his mother's cries and pleas going unheard, until finally, eventually, he heard the familiar mantra, the mantra he knew by heart, even as his mother continued to sob. Over and over he heard his father utter the words telling her he was sorry, telling her he loved her. 'Signome! Se agapo. Se agapo poli. Signome.'

Sam! Eve woke with a mother's certainty that something was wrong, bolting from the bed and momentarily disoriented with her new surroundings, only to realise it wasn't Sam who was in trouble. For in the bed she'd so recently left, Leo was thrashing from side to side, making gravel-voiced mutterings against the mattress, rantings that made no sense in any language she knew, his body glossy with sweat under the moonlight.

He cried out in his sleep, a howl of desperation and helplessness, anguish clear in his tortured limbs and fevered brow as he twisted and writhed. Eve did the only thing she could think of, the only thing she knew helped Sam when he had night terrors. She went to Leo's side of the bed and sat down softly. 'It's okay, Leo,' she said, sweeping a calming hand over his brow, finding it burning hot. He flnched at her touch, resisting it at first, so she tried to soothe him with her words. 'It's okay. It's all right. You're safe now. Leo, you're safe.'

He seemed to slump under her hands, his body slick with sweat, his breathing still hard but slowing, and Eve suspected that whatever demons had invaded his midnight hours had now departed. She went to leave then, to return to her side of the bed, but when she made a move to leave, a hand locked around her wrist and she realised that maybe there were still some demons hanging on.

And just as she would do and had done with Sam when he needed comfort, she slid under the covers alongside the hot body of Leo, putting her arm around him, soothing him back to sleep with the gentle reassurance of another's touch and trying not to think of the heated presence lying so close to her or the thud of his heart under her hands.

Five minutes should be enough, she figured, until he had settled back into sleep. Five minutes and she'd escape back to her edge of the mattress. Five minutes would be more than enough…

* * *

Something was different. She woke to the soft light of the coming dawn, filtering grey through the shutters, and to the sound of birdsong coming from the palms outside. And she woke to the certain knowledge that she had stayed far, far too long. Fingers trailed over her back, making lazy circles on her skin through her thin cotton nightie and setting her skin to tingling, and warm lips nuzzled at her brow as the hand between them somehow managed to brush past her nipples and send spears of electricity to her core.

And she was very, very aroused.

She was also trapped, his heavy arm over her, one leg casually thrown over hers. She tried to wiggle her way out but the movement brought her into contact with a part of him that told her he was also very much aroused. He growled his appreciation, shifted closer, and she tried not to think about how good that part of him had felt inside her.

'Leo…' she said, conflicted, her mind in panic, her body in revolt, turning her face up to his, only to be met by his mouth as he dragged her into his long, lazy kiss, a kiss she had no power or intention to cut short even though she knew it was utter madness.

Utter pleasure.

Her senses soared, her flesh tingled and breasts ached for the caress of his clever hands and hot mouth, and arguments that things were complicated enough, that there was no point, that this must end and end badly made little impression against this slow, sensual onslaught.

'I see you changed your mind,' he murmured, a brush of velvet against her skin.

'You had a nightmare.'

'This,' he said, sliding one long-fingered hand up the back of her leg, kneading her bottom in his hand, 'is no nightmare.'

'Don't you—' His mouth cut her off again as his hand captured her breast, working at her nipple, plucking at her nerve endings, making her groan into his mouth with the exquisite pleasure of his caress, emerging breathless and dizzy when it ended so that she almost forgot what she wanted to say. 'Don't you remember?'

'Maybe…' he said, rolling her under him, pinning her arms to the bed above her head as his head dipped to her throat, 'maybe right now I'd rather forget.'

She moaned with the wicked pleasure of it all, his hot mouth like a brand against her skin. But this wasn't supposed to happen. She hadn't wanted this to happen. But as he lowered his head to her breast and drew in one achingly hard nipple to his mouth, laving it with his hot tongue, blowing on the damp fabric and sending exquisite chills coursing through her, she couldn't, for the life of her, remember why. Her body was alive with wanting him, alive with the power that came from him and that she craved, and there was no way she could stop.

He let her wrists go, his hands busy at her nightie. She felt the soft fabric lifting as he skimmed his hands up her sides, before skimming down again, taking her underwear with them. 'You're beautiful,' he growled, his voice like a brush of velvet over her bare skin as he pulled it over her head. And yet he was the magnificent one, broad and dark, his erection swaying and bucking over her, a pearl of liquid glistening at its head. Transfixed, unable to stop herself, she reached out her hand and touched it with the pad of her thumb. He uttered something urgent, his dark eyes flared, wild and filled with the same dark need that consumed her as he swiped up his wallet, found what he needed and tossed the wallet away in his rush to be inside her.

He dragged in air, forced himself to slow. 'You do this to me,' he accused her softly as he parted her thighs with his hand and found her slick and wet and wanting. 'You make me rock hard and aching,' he continued, his fingers circling that tiny nub of nerve endings, a touch so delicious she mewled with pleasure, writhing as sensation built on the back of his words, fuelling her need, fuelling her desperation.

Until at last she felt him nudge her *there*, hot and hard and pulsing with life as he tensed above her for one tantalising moment of anticipation.

And then joyfully, blissfully, he entered her in one magical thrust and she held him there, at her very core, welcoming him home, tears squeezing from her eyes at the sheer ecstasy of it all.

So much to feel. So much to experience and hold precious. And still the best was to come.

The dance, the friction, the delicious moment of tension when he would sit poised at her entrance, before slamming back inside.

She went with him, matched him measure for measure, gasp for gasp as the pace increased, their bodies slick and hot as the rhythm increased, faster, more furious, the climb too high until this thing building inside her felt too big for her chest, her lungs too small.

Until with one final thrust, one final guttural roar, he sent her shattering, coming apart in his arms, falling, spinning weightless and formless and satisfied beyond measure.

'So beautiful,' he said, as he smoothed her hair from her damp brow, kissing her lightly on her eyes, on her nose, on her gasping lips.

And you're dangerous, she thought as he disappeared to the bathroom, as her brain resumed functioning and a cold and very real panic seized her heart. So utterly, utterly dangerous.

And I am so in trouble.

What should one say now? What would an army do, its defences stripped bare, the castle walls well and truly breached? Try to hastily re-build them? Call for reinforcements?

Or surrender?

She squeezed her eyes shut, trying not to think about the sizzle under her skin where his fingers had stroked her shoulder.

As if she had a choice. She would no sooner patch up her defences and he would have them down again. One silken touch, one poignant kiss, and he would have those walls tumbling right down.

But she was kidding himself. There was no point rebuilding walls or calling for reinforcements. No point trying to save herself from attack from outside the castle walls.

Not when the enemy was already within.

Tears sprang to her eyes and she swiped them away. Damn. What was she doing? What was she risking? 'I can't afford to get pregnant again,' she said when he returned, putting voice to her greatest fear.

'I wouldn't let you.'

'But Sam's father—'

He rose over her, cutting her off with his kiss. 'I would never do that to you.'

'How do I know that? And I would have two babies from two different fathers. How could I cope with that?'

'Believe me. It won't happen but even if it did, I would not abandon you as he has done.'

'But you wouldn't marry me either.'

He searched her eyes and frowned and she thought it was at her words, until he used the pad of his thumb to wipe away the moisture there.

'I thought I heard you say any woman would be certifiably insane to want to get shackled to me.'

'I'm sorry,' she whispered, remembering the scene in the bar. 'I was angry.'

'As was I. I should never have said what I did about Sam's father thinking the same of you. But you're right. Marriage is not an option, which means the best thing for everyone is to ensure we're careful. All right?'

She wished he wouldn't be like this. She wished he could go back to being ruthless and hard, because when he was tender and gentle with her, she could almost, *almost*, imagine he actually cared.

And she could almost, *almost*, imagine that she cared for him. She couldn't afford to care for him. She couldn't afford to read anything into his apology for what he'd said about Sam's dad when it was plain he wasn't lining up to marry her himself.

But she could enjoy him.

Two more nights in Leo's bed. Why was she fighting it when it was where she so wanted to be? Why not treat it as the holiday it really was? Time spent in a tropical paradise with a man who knew how to pleasure a woman. No ties, no commitments and a promise not to let her down.

Was she mad to fight it?

And was it really surrendering, to take advantage of what she'd been offered on a plate?

His hand cupped her breast, feeling its weight, stroking her nipple and her senses until it peaked hard and plump under his fingers while his lips worked their heated way along her jaw towards her mouth. 'Evelyn?'

A woman would have to be mad to want to give

this up, she reasoned, leaning into his ministrations, giving herself over to the sensations. Two nights to enjoy the pleasures of the flesh. It was more than some people had in a lifetime.

It would be enough.

It had to be enough.

'All right,' she whispered, giving herself up to his kiss.

CHAPTER TEN

SAM'S morning chatter roused them, as he tested all the sounds in his vocabulary in one long gabble, then she heard a tell-tale bump on the floor, followed by a squeal. 'That's Sam,' she said unnecessarily, locating her nightie and snatching up her balled-up underwear and a robe and making for the bathroom for a quick pit stop, wanting to ensure she looked maternal rather than wanton when she greeted her son. Not that he was old enough to notice anything amiss, she thought, giving thanks for his innocence.

Sam was hanging onto the rails and bouncing on the mattress and greeted her with a huge grin followed by 'mumumumumum', which warmed her heart. Unconditional love. There was nothing like it. She changed him on the table provided and equipped for the task before popping his wriggling body down on the floor. 'Bear!' he shouted, gleefully scooping up the toy and running with his wide toddler gait out of the room before her, looking a little bit lost at the new surroundings for just a moment, before running full pelt and colliding with the bed.

Dark eyes blinked up at Leo, openly curious. He blinked back, wondering what one was supposed to say to a child. Sam looked around at his mother, who was pulling milk from the fridge in the small kitchenette and pouring it into a jug. 'It's okay, Sam, you remember Leo,' she said reassuringly as she put the jug in the microwave, and Sam turned and careened straight into his mother's legs, hiding his face between them.

'I'm sorry,' she said, hoisting him to her hip in one efficient movement, although it wasn't so much the efficiency that impressed Leo but the unexpected way the sudden angle of her hip displayed the long line of her legs. His mouth went dry, his blood went south. Strange really, for here she was, dressed in a cheap cotton nightgown, a toweling robe sashed at her waist and with a baby at her hip, and maybe it was her tousled hair, or the jut of that damned hip, or even the fact she'd just blown his world apart in bed—twice—but suddenly he was thinking about a third time.

The microwave pinged.

'Ping,' cried Sam, holding his hands out. 'Ping!'

One-handed, she poured the milk into some kind of cup, fixing on a spout before passing it to the boy. 'Here's your ping, Sam.' Leo watched her, admiring the way she looked so at ease working one-handedly. Sam dropped his bear to clasp the cup in his pudgy hands, gulping deep. 'Sam's used to joining me in bed in the morning,' she said, bending over to retrieve the bear and giving his sex a hell of a jolt in the process. Until, through the fog of rising testosterone, it occurred to him that she was about to bring Sam back to bed.

'Although, admittedly,' she added, already on her way, 'he's not used to finding someone else there.'

He tucked that piece of information away in a file that came marked with a tick, even as he gladly took her hint and pulled on a robe to vacate the bed. He liked the knowledge she didn't often entertain at home. Sam was evidence she'd been with someone, and that wasn't something he wanted to contemplate. He didn't want to think there had been or were others.

'I didn't mean you had to run away,' she said, settling Sam between the pillows. 'It's still early.'

'I think I'll go for a run.'

'You haven't had that much to do with babies or children, have you?'

'Does it show?'

'Blatantly. You might want to do something about that if you want people to believe you're actually Sam's father. The fact you're travelling most of the year is no excuse for not knowing how to deal with the child who's supposed to be your own.'

He shrugged, knowing he'd handled things badly last night, not even remembering his supposed son's age, but uncomfortable with where the conversation was headed. 'What do you suggest?'

'Maybe you should try holding him from time to time. Even just hold his hand. Engage with him.'

'Engage with him?'

'He's a person, Leo, just like anyone else. Maybe try directing all that animal magnetism you have at him instead of every woman you happen to meet.'

He looked at the child. Looked back at her, not sure who was making him feel more uncomfortable now. 'But can he even understand what I say?'

She laughed. 'More than you know.'

He sat down awkwardly on the side of the bed, watching Sam, Sam watching him as he swigged at his milk, his teddy tucked securely once again under his arm.

And Sam guzzled the last of his milk and held out his toy. 'Bear!'

He looked on uncertainly, not sure what was expected of him, unfamiliar with this role. 'I'm not sure I can do this.'

'He's offering it to you. Try taking it,' she suggested.

He put out his hand toward the bear and Sam immediately rolled over, giggling madly, the toy wedged tightly beneath him.

He looked over at her. 'I don't get it.'

'It's a game, Leo. Wait.' And sure enough the arm shot out again.

'Bear.'

This time Leo made a grab for it. A slow lunge, and way too slow for Sam, but he loved it anyway, squealing with glee as he hid his teddy.

The next time was nearly a draw, Sam winning by a whisker, and he was in stitches on the bed, his body curved over his prize, and even Leo was finding it amusing. 'He's quick,' he said, and he looked at Evelyn, who was smiling too, although her eyes looked almost sad, almost as if…

'I'll go take a shower,' he said, standing abruptly, not interested in analysing what a look like that might mean. He didn't do family. He'd told her that. And if the shadowed remnants of last night's nightmares had reminded him of him anything, it was that he could never do family. He dared not risk it. He was broken, and that was just the way it was.

So she could look at him any damned way and it would make no difference. Because after two more nights with her, he would let her go for ever.

He didn't want anything more.

And he definitely didn't want her pity.

They were all meeting after breakfast at the dock, ready for a day's adventure. A morning sail, and then a helicopter trip over the more far-flung sights of the islands and the reef. Hannah had already collected Sam and taken him up to the main house where there was a large playroom filled with toys and games and all surrounded by secure fences so he couldn't get into trouble if he wandered off. Which meant Eve had a rare few hours without Sam, not to work but to enjoy her beautiful if temporary surroundings, and the heated attention of a man just as beautiful and temporary, if a lot more complex.

He held her hand as they wended their way along the palm-studded sand toward the dock on the bay, the whispering wind promising a day of seductive warmth, the odd scattered white cloud offering no threat, and the man at her side promising days and nights filled with sinful pleasures.

Now that she had made her decision, and had Leo's commitment that he wouldn't abandon her if the worst happened, as Sam's father had done, she was determined to enjoy every last moment of it. Maybe she was crazy, but she trusted him, at least on that score. And there was no question that he didn't lack the means to support a child.

The morning sun kissed her bare arms where it infiltrated the foliage, the air fresh with salt and the sweet scent of tropical flowers. Ten whole degrees warmer up here than Melbourne's showery forecast, Eve had heard when she'd flicked on the weather channel while feeding Sam his breakfast. She could think of worse ways to spend the time waiting for a new hot water service to be installed.

She glanced up at the man alongside her, his loose white shirt rolled up at the cuffs, with designer stubble adding to his pirate appeal, and with one look the memories of their love-making flooded back, warming her in places the sun did not reach. Oh, no, she would have no trouble enjoying her nights with him either.

'You look pleased with yourself.'

'Do I?' Only then did she realise she'd been smiling. 'It must be the weather.'

'Good morning!' Maureen said, greeting them, looking resort elegant in linen co-ordinates in taupe and coffee colours. 'How was the bure? Did you all sleep well?'

Eve smiled. 'It's just beautiful. I love it here.'

'Everything is perfect,' Leo added, slipping an arm around Eve's shoulders, giving her arm a squeeze. 'Couldn't be better.'

'And Sam's okay with Hannah? You're not worried about leaving him, are you?'

Eve shook her head. 'Hannah's wonderful. He's having the time of his life.'

The older woman looked from one to the other and smiled knowingly. 'I hope you understand why we were so keen to drag you away from Melbourne. And there's just so much more to share with you.'

'All aboard!' called Eric, appropriately wearing a captain's cap over his silvering hair, and Leo handed both women onto the yacht where Richard and Felicity were already waiting. There was a distinct holiday mood in the air as they set off, the boat slicing through the azure waters, the wind catching in the flapping sails, the magnificent vistas ever-changing, with new wonders revealed around every point, with every new bay. 'Isn't it fabulous?' Felicity said, leaning over the railing, looking glamorous in a short wrap skirt and peasant top, and Eve could't help but agree, even though she felt decidedly designer dull in her denim shorts and chain-store tank-top. Motherhood in Melbourne, she reflected, didn't lend itself to a vast resort wardrobe.

Decidedly dull, that was, until Leo slipped an arm around her waist and pressed his mouth to her ear. 'Did I tell you how much I love your shorts,' he whispered, 'and how much I can't wait to peel them off?'

And she shuddered right there in anticipation of that very act. But first there were other pleasures, other discoveries. They discovered secret bays and tiny coves with sheer cliff walls and crystal-clear waters. They found bays where inlets carved dark blue ribbons through shallow water backed by pure white sand, a thousand shades of blue and green against the stark white beach and the lushly vegetated hills rising above.

They stopped for a swim at that beach, followed

by a picnic comprising a large platter of antipasto and cold chicken and prawns, with Vietnamese cold rolls with dipping sauce all washed down with chilled white wine or sparkling water.

After lunch, the Alvarezes went for a stroll along the beach and Maureen took a snooze while Eric and Leo chatted, no doubt about business, a little way away. And Eve was happy to sit right there on the beach in her bikini, taking in the wonders of the scenery around her, the islands and the mountains, the lush foliage and amazing sea and above it all the endless blue sky. And she felt guilty for not sharing it with Sam, even though she knew that if he had come, none of them would have been able to relax for a minute. One day, when he was older, she would love to show him.

Leo dropped down on his knees behind her, picked up her bottle of lotion and squeezed some into his hand, started smoothing it onto her shoulders and neck until she almost purred with pleasure. She didn't think it necessary to inform him she'd just done that. 'You look deep in thought.'

'I was just thinking how much Sam would love this. I'll have to try to bring him one day.'

His hands stilled for a moment, before they resumed their slippery, sensual massage. 'Don't you love it?' she said. 'Can you believe the colour of that sea?'

'I've seen it before.'

'You have?' But of course he would have. Leo had been everywhere. 'Where?'

'In your eyes.'

The shiver arrowed directly down her spine. She snapped her head round. 'What?'

He squeezed more lotion, spread it down her arms, his fingertips brushing her bikini top as he looked out at the bay. 'When I first saw them, they reminded me of the Aegean, of the sea around the islands of Santorini and Mykonos, but I was wrong. For every colour in your eyes is right here, in these waters.'

And that battle scarred never-say-die, foolish, foolish creature inside her lumbered back into life and prepared for take-off once more. 'Leo...'

He looked down at her upturned face, touched

one hand to the side of her face. 'I don't know how I'm ever going to forget those eyes.'

Then don't! she almost blurted, surprising herself with her vehement reaction, but he angled her shoulders and invited her into his kiss, a heart-wrenching bitter-sweet kiss that spoke of something lost before it had even been found, and she cursed a man with a stone for a heart, cursed her own foolish heart for caring.

'Come on, you two lovebirds,' Eric yelled along the beach. 'We've got a seaplane to catch!'

If the Whitsundays had been spectacular from the boat, they were breathtaking from the air in the clear afternoon light. Island after island could be explored from the air in the tiny plane, each island a brilliant green gem in a sapphire sea. And just when Eve thought it couldn't possibly get any better, they headed out over the Coral Sea to the Great Barrier Reef. The sheer scale of the reefs took everyone's breath away, the colours vivid and bright, like someone had painted pictures upon the sea, random shapes bordered in snowy white splashed with everything from emerald green and palest blue to muted shades of mocha.

And then they landed on the water and transferred to a glass-bottomed boat so they could see the amazing Technicolor world under the sea together with its rich sea life. 'I am definitely coming back one day to show Sam,' she told Maureen as they boarded the seaplane for the journey back to Mina. 'Thank you so much for today. I know I'll treasure these memories for ever.'

And from the back seat Eric piped up, 'You just wait. We saved the best till last!'

They had. They were heading back over a section he identified as Hardy Reef, one part of a network of reefs that extended more than two thousand kilometres up the north Queensland coastline, when she saw something that didn't fit with the randomness of the coral structures.

She pointed out the window. 'That looks like… Is that what I think it is?' Eric laughed and had the pilot circle around so they could all see.

'That's it. What do you think of that?'

It was incredible and for a moment her brain

had refused to believe what her eyes were telling her. For in the middle of a kind of lagoon in the midst of a coral reef where everything appeared random, there sat a reef grown in the shape of a heart, its outline made from coral that looked from above like milk chocolate sprinkles on a cake, the inside like it was covered in a soft cream-cheese frosting, all surrounded by a sea of brilliant blue.

And little wonder she thought in terms of frostings and cakes, because it reminded her so much of the cake she'd made for Sam for his first birthday, knowing that as he got older he'd want bears or trains or some cartoon character or other. She figured that for his first, before he had a say, she could choose, and she'd made a heart shape, because that was what Sam meant to her.

'Look, Richard,' Felicity said, clasping his hand as they circled around. 'It's a heart. Isn't that amazing?'

'It magical,' Eve said, gazing down in wonder at the unique formation below. 'This entire place is just magical. Thank you.' The Culshaws laughed, delighted with the reactions of their guests as

Leo took her hand and pressed it to his lips. She turned to him, surprised at the tenderness of the gesture, finding his eyes softly sad, feeling that sense of loss again, for something she had not yet quite gained. 'What is it?' she asked, confused.

'You are magical,' he told her, and his words shimmied down her spine and left her infused with a warm, golden glow and a question mark over her earlier accusation. A heart of stone? she wondered.

But there was definitely something magical in the air.

They dined alfresco that evening, an informal barbecue held early enough that Sam could join them, happily showing off his new toy collection to anyone who displayed an interest. Luckily nobody seemed to mind and Sam was in his element, lapping up the attention. When he yawned, there was general consensus amongst the couples. It had been a fabulous day, but exhausting, and tomorrow there was serious work to be done, an agreement to finally be hammered out between the men, a morning at the spa on a neighbouring island for the women.

And before that a night of explosive sex. Eve felt the tension change in the man alongside her, the barely restrained desire bubbling away so close to the surface she could just about smell the pheromones on the fresh night air. She sensed the changes in her own body, the prickling aware-ness, the mounting heat. It distracted her.

Sam, sensing the party winding up around him, found his second wind and made a dash for the toy room. Eve was too slow, caught un-awares, and surprised when it was Felicity who snatched up the squirming child. 'Gotcha!' she said, swinging him in the air and tickling his tummy before, breathless and red cheeked, she passed him to his mother.

He was asleep before they reached the bure. She put Sam down, emerging from his small room to a darkened bedroom, lit only by the moonlight filtering through the glass windows. Leo had left the blinds open. She liked that; liked the way the shadows of the palms swayed on the breeze; liked the way the room glowed silver.

'Come to bed,' came the velvet-clad invitation. And that was the part she liked best of all.

She was screaming again, crying out in pain as the blows rained down, as the bad words contin-ued. 'Stomato to!' *he cried from his bed.* 'Stop it!' *But it didn't stop, and in fear and desperation he crept to the door, tears streaming down his face, afraid to move, afraid not to move, afraid of what he would find when he opened the door. So he did nothing, just curled up into a ball behind the door and covered his ears and prayed for it to stop.*

'Leo, it's okay.'

He sat bolt upright in bed, panting, desperate for air, burning up. He put his hands to his head, bent over his knees.

'You had a nightmare again.'

God, it wasn't a nightmare. *It was his life.* He swept the sheet aside, stormed from the bed, pacing the floor, circuit after circuit.

Twenty years ago he had escaped. Twenty years ago he had made his own way. But he had always known it was there, always known it was lurking. Waiting.

But it had never been this close. This real.

He felt cool hands on his back. 'What is it?'

He flinched, jumping away. 'Don't touch me! You shouldn't touch me!'

'Leo?'

'I have to go for a walk.' He pulled open a drawer, pulled out a pair of cotton pants and shoved his legs into them.

'It's two o'clock in the morning.'

'Let me go!'

The night air fanned around him, warming against his burning skin, the shallows sucking at his feet. There was a reason he didn't get close to anyone. Good reason. He was broken. Twisted. Made to be alone.

Couldn't she see that?

And yet she kept looking at him that way with those damned blue eyes and even had him wishing for things that could never be. It was his fault. When had he stopped acting a part? When had he forgotten that this weekend was about pretence, that it wasn't real?

When she'd bucked underneath him in bed, her body writhing in its sweat-slicked release? Or when she'd talked about her parents and made him want to reach out and soothe her pain?

He stopped where the beach turned to rock, looked out over the sea to the looming dark shapes of the nearest islands.

One more day. One more night. And he would take her home before he could hurt her and there would be no more dreams.

It was as easy and as hard as that.

CHAPTER ELEVEN

SHE needed this. Eve lay on the massage table, scented candles perfuming the air, skilful hands working the knots out of her back and neck. She only wished someone would work out the knots in her mind, but that was impossible while Leo Zamos was at their core.

He'd been so desperate to get away, bursting from the bure this morning like the devil himself was after him. She'd watched him go, lit by moonlight as he'd moved through the trees towards the beach. Watched him and waited for him to come back. But eventually she'd gone back to bed and when she'd woken, he'd been sitting, having coffee on the deck.

She didn't know what it was, only that something was terribly, desperately wrong and that if he only opened up and shared what was troubling him, maybe she could help.

She sighed, a mixture of muscular bliss and frustrated mind, as the masseuse had her roll over, readying her for her facial. What was the point of wanting to help? He didn't want it and tomorrow she would go home, and all of this would be nothing more than a memory.

She couldn't afford to care. She mustn't, even when he told her she was magical. Even when he tugged on her heart and her soul with his kiss.

Even though she so very much wanted to believe it.

Thoroughly pampered after their hours at the spa, the three women enjoyed a late lunch at the big house, on the terrace overlooking the pool. The men were still in conference apparently, although Maureen suggested that might just mean they'd popped out in the boat for a spot of fishing while the women weren't looking. Not that it mattered. After they'd been massaged until their bones had just about melted, they were more than content to sit and chat in the warm, balmy air of tropical North Queensland. After all, they were going home tomorrow. Soon enough real life would intrude.

Sam was once again more than happy to provide the entertainment if they weren't up to it. He tottered between the three women, perfectly at ease with them all now, sharing around building blocks he'd taken a shine to, taking them back and redistributing them as if this was all part of some grand plan, happily chattering the whole time. Eve watched him, so proud of her little man, knowing that at least when Leo walked out of her life, she would still have Sam. He'd surprised her too. Instead of providing a disruptive force, as she'd expected, it seemed that, at least in some part, he seemed to pull them together. He definitely kept them amused.

And Felicity surprised her again, playing his games, picking him up when he passed, giving him hugs and raspberry kisses on his cheek to his squeals and giggles of delight before he scampered off on his toddler legs.

'I always wanted a child,' she said wistfully, her eyes following his escape. 'In fact, I always imagined myself surrounded by children. And when I met Richard and thought he was the one, I thought it might happen, even though it was already getting late...' Then she blinked and looked around. 'I guess things sometimes turn out differently to what we expect.'

And the other two women nodded, each wrapped in their own separate thoughts and experiences.

'It seemed easier to give up and pretend it didn't matter. But meeting you and seeing you with Sam makes me realise how much it means to me. I want to try again. At least one more time.' Tears made her eyes glassy. 'You're so lucky to be able to give Leo a child, Evelyn. I really wish I could do the same for Richard.' Her voice hitched. 'Damn! I'm so sorry.' She fled inside.

Eve felt sick, a hand instinctively going to her mouth. And all the good feelings, all the positive goodwill she'd been stashing away in her memory while she was determined to enjoy this weekend were for nothing. They meant nothing if her deceit led someone else to want what she was having. A wish based on a lie.

She rose to follow and tell her exactly that when Maureen stopped her. 'Let her go.'

'But she thinks—'

Maureen nodded. 'I know what she thinks.'

'But you don't understand.' She slumped back in her chair, feeling the weight of the lie crushing down on her, feeling her heart squeezed tight, knowing she couldn't go home without admitting the truth. 'I hate this! I hate the pretence. I'm so sorry, Maureen.' She shook her head, and still couldn't find a nice way to say it. 'Look, Leo's not really Sam's father.'

She heard a sharp intake of air, followed by an equally sharp exhalation. But then, instead of the censure she'd expected, or the outrage, she felt a gentling hand over her own. 'I wondered when you were going to feel able to share that.'

Warily, feeling sicker than ever, Eve looked up. 'You knew?'

'From the moment I met you in that bar in Melbourne. Of course, Sam could have passed for Leo's son, but it was crystal clear to anyone who had ever been a mother that Leo had no idea about being a father. And then his awkwardness at dinner, not knowing his own son's birthday, only reinforced that impression, at least to me.'

She shrugged. 'Though when it comes down to it, does Sam's parentage really matter?'

'But you don't understand. It's not that simple—'

'Of course it's that simple.' Maureen said, cutting her off. 'I saw you and Leo out there yesterday in the boat and on the beach. It's clear to everyone that you love him and he loves you, so why should it matter one bit who Sam's father really is?' she insisted. 'Why should a silly detail like that matter when you are going to marry a man who clearly worships the ground you walk on? Now, I'll go check on Felicity and you stop worrying.'

How could Maureen know so much and yet be so wrong? Eve sat on the sand with Sam, watching him busily digging holes. All those hours of massaging and jet baths and a relaxing facial, all that pampering and all for nothing. Not even the magic of the island itself, the rustle of the palms and the vivid colours, none of it could dispel the tightness in her gut.

She didn't love Leo.

Sure, she was worried about him and whatever it was that plagued his dreams and turned his skin cold with sweat, and she certainly had an unhealthy obsession with the man, one that had started that fateful day three years ago, and which had only gathered momentum after mind-blowing nights of sex.

And maybe she didn't want to to think about going home tomorrow and never seeing him again.

But that was hardly the same as love.

As for Leo, no way did he love her. He was merely acting a part, plying her with attention as a means to an end, certainly not because he loved her. Ridiculous. They'd only been together a couple of days after all. What Maureen was witnessing was pure lust. Leo just had a bit more to throw around than most. He didn't do family and he didn't want her thinking he'd change his mind. Why else would he underline every endearment, every tender moment with a stinging reminder that it would soon end?

Sam oohed and pulled something from the sand then, shaking it, showing her what looked like some kind of shell, and she gave up thinking about questions she had no answers to, puzzles that made no sense. Tomorrow, she knew, she would go home and this brief interlude in her life would be over and she would have to find herself new clients and build a new fee base. And look after Sam. That's what she should be worrying about.

'Shall we see what it is, Sam?' she said to the child, a launch catching her attention for just a moment as it powered past the bay, before taking Sam's hand as they stepped into the shallows to wash this new treasure clean.

'Boat!' he said, pointing.

'It is,' she said. 'A big one.'

Her sarong clung to her where she'd sat in the damp sand, her ankles looked lean and sexy as her feet were lapped by the shallows, all her attention on her child by her side, guiding him, encouraging him with just a touch or a word or a smile, and he knew in that instant he had never seen anything more beautiful or powerful or sexy.

All he knew was that he wanted her. He wanted to celebrate, knowing the deal was finally done, but he wanted something more fundamental too. More basic. More necessary.

Except he also knew he couldn't let that happen. He'd realised that during his walk this morning and as much as he'd tried to find a way around it all day, even when he was supposed to be thinking about the Culshaw deal, he still knew it to be true. He couldn't take the chance.

He watched, as mother and son washed something in the shallows, he couldnt tell what, and she must have sensed his presence because he hadn't moved and she couldn't have heard him, yet she'd turned her head and looked up and seen him. And he'd seen his name on her lips as she'd stood and she'd smiled, only a tentative smile, but after the way he'd abandoned her this morning, he didn't deserve even that much.

And something bent and shifted and warmed inside that he could treat her so badly and still she could find a smile for him. He hoped it meant she liked him, just a little, just enough to one day find a way to forgive him for the way he had no choice but to treat her.

The wash was nothing really. No more than a ripple to any adult, and Leo had no idea it would be any different for a child, until he saw Sam pushed face first into the water with the rolling force of it.

'Sam!' he yelled, crossing the beach and pulling the child, spluttering and then squealing, from the water. 'Is he all right?' he asked, as she collected the wailing child, dropping to her towel, rocking him on her shoulder.

'Oh, my God, I took my eye off him for a second,' she said, her voice heavy with self-recrimination. 'I'm so sorry, Sam,' she said, kissing his head. 'I should have seen that coming.'

'Will he be okay?' Leo asked, but Sam's cries were already abating. He sniffled and hiccuped and caught sight of a passing sail, twisting in his mother's arms as his arm shot out. 'Boat!'

She sighed with relief. 'He sounds fine. He got a shock. I think we all did.'

Leo squatted down beside them and they said nothing for a while, all watching the boat bob by.

'You actually picked him up,' she said. 'Is that the first time you've ever held a child?'

He frowned as he considered her question, not because he didn't already know the answer but because this weekend suddenly seemed filled with firsts: the first time he'd thought a cotton nightie sexy; the first time he'd looked at a woman holding a baby and got a hard on; the first time he'd felt remorse that he'd never see a particular woman again…

But, no, he wasn't going there. What were his nightmares if not a warning of what would happen if he did?

'It's not something my job calls for much of, no.'

'Well, thank you for acting so quickly. I don't know what I was doing.'

He knew. She'd been looking at him with those damned eyes of hers. And he hadn't wanted to let them go.

Sam soon grew restless in his mother's arms and wiggled his way out, soon scouring the sands and collecting new treasure, keeping a healthy distance from the water, his mother shadowing his every movement.

'So how goes the deal?'

'It's done.'

She looked up, her expression unreadable, and he wasn't entirely certain what he'd been looking for. 'Congratulations. You must be pleased.'

'It's a good feeling.' Strangely, though, it didn't feel as good as it usually did, didn't feel as good as he'd expected it would. Maybe because of all the delays.

And then she was suddenly squatting down, writing Sam's name with a stick in the sand while he looked on, clapping. 'So we're done here.'

And that didn't make him feel any better. 'Looks like it. Culshaw is planning a celebratory dinner for tonight and tomorrow we all go home.'

'I thought you didn't have a home.'

There was a lump in the back of his throat that shouldn't have been there. He was supposed to be feeling good about this, wasn't he? He rubbed the back of his neck with his hand, watched her write 'Mum' in the sand. 'Mum,' she said to Sam, pointing.

Sam leaned over with his hands on his pudgy knees and solemnly studied the squiggles she'd made in the sand. 'Mumumumum,' sang Sam.

'That's right, clever clogs, you can read!' And she gave him a big squeeze that he wriggled out of and scooted off down the beach.

'Tell me about Sam's father,' Leo said, as they followed along behind.

She looked up suspiciously, her eyebrows jagging in the middle. Where was this coming from? 'Why?'

'Who was he?'

She shrugged. 'Just some guy I met.'

'You don't strike me as the "just-some-guy-I-met" type.'

'Oh, and you, with your vast experience of women, you'd know about all the different types, I guess.'

'Stop trying to change the subject. This is about you. How did you manage to hook up with such a loser?'

She stopped then, her eyes flicking between

Leo and Sam. 'You don't know the first thing about me. And you certainly don't know the first thing about him. He just turned out not to be who I thought he was.'

'I know that he was a fool to let you go.'

Wow, she thought, forced to close her eyes for a second as the tremor rattled through her, *where did that come from*?

'Thanks,' she said, still getting over his last comment. 'But it was me who was the fool.'

'For getting pregnant? You can't blame yourself for that.'

For ever imagining he was anything at all like Leo. 'No. For believing him. He was an interstate consultant who visited every couple of weeks. Always flirting. We worked late one night, he invited me out for a drink afterwards'—*and he had sexy dark hair and olive skin and dark eyes and I wanted to pretend...*

'And?'

She shrugged. 'And the rest, as they say, is history.'

'You told him about Sam—about the pregnancy?'

'I told him. I wasn't particularly interested in seeing him again, but I thought he had a right to know. He wasn't interested as it happened. He was more interested in his wife not finding out.'

'Scum!' he spat, surprising her with the level of ferocity behind the word.

'It's not so bad. At least I've got Sam. And it got me motivated to start my own business.' She caught a flash of movement in the crystal clear water, a school of tiny fish darting to and fro in the shallows. She scooped up her son and ventured to the water's edge, careful not to disturb them. 'Look Sam,' she said, 'fish!'

And Sam's eyes opened wide, his arms pumping up and down. 'Fith!'

She laughed, chasing the fish in the shallows even as she envied her young son his raw enthusiasm. She envied him his simple needs and pleasures. Why did it have to become so hard when you were a grown up, she wondered, when the world spun not on the turns of the planet and shades of dark or light, but on emotions that made a mockery of science and fact and good sense.

Wanting Leo was so not good sense.

Loving him made even less.

Maureen was wrong. She had to be.

The mood at dinner was jovial, the conversation flowing and fun. Only Leo seemed tense, strangely separate from the group, as if he'd already moved on to the next place, the next deal. The next woman. 'Are you all right?' she asked, on the way back to their bure, his hand like a vise around hers. 'Do you want to go take a walk first?'

Hannah had taken Sam back earlier and by now he would be safely in the land of Nod. They didn't have to rush back if he had something on his mind.

He blew out in a rush. 'I'll sleep on the sofa tonight,' he said almost too quickly, as if the words had been waiting to spill out. 'It'll be better that way.'

And she stopped right where she was and refused to move on so he had no choice but to turn and face her. 'You're telling me that after three nights of the best sex of my life, on the last night we have together, you're going to sleep on the sofa? Not a chance.'

He tried to smile. Failed miserably. 'It's for the best.'

'Who says? What's wrong, Leo? Why can't you tell me?'

'Believe me,' he snorted, 'you really don't want to know.'

'I wouldn't ask if I didn't want to know. What the hell changes tonight? The fact you don't have to pretend anymore?'

'You think I ever had to pretend about that?'

'Then don't pretend you don't want me tonight.' She moved closer, ran her free hand up his chest, 'We've got just one night left together. We're good together. You said that yourself. Why can't we enjoy it?'

He grabbed her hand, pushed it away. 'Don't you understand? It's for your own good!'

'How can I believe that if you won't tell me? What's wrong? Is it the dreams you're having?'

And he made a roar like a wounded animal in distress, a cry that spoke of so much pain and anguish and loss that it chilled her to the bone. 'Just leave it,' he said. 'Just leave me.'

He turned and stormed off across the sand towards the beach, leaving her standing there, gutted and empty on the path.

Maybe it was better this way, she thought, as she dragged herself back to the bure, forcing herself to put on a bright face for Hannah who wasn't taken in for a moment, she could tell, but she wasn't about to explain it to anyone. Not when she had no idea what was happening herself.

She checked Sam, listening to his even breathing, giving thanks for the fact he was in her life, giving thanks for the gift she'd been given, even if borne of a mistake. He was the best mistake she'd ever made.

And then she dragged bedding to the sofa, knowing from the previous night Leo was more likely to disturb her if he tried to fit onto the sofa than because of any nightmare he might have. At least she knew he would fit on the big king sized bed.

She lay there in the dark, waiting for what

seemed like hours, until at last she heard his foot-fall on the decking outside. She cracked open her eyelids as the sliding door swooshed open and she saw his silhouette framed in the door-way, big and dark and not dangerous, like she'd always seen him, but strangely sad. He crossed the floor softly, hesitating when he got to the sofa. She could hear him at her feet, hear his troubled breathing.

Come to me, she willed, *pick me up and carry me to bed like you have done before and make love to me.*

And she heard him turn on a sigh and move away. She heard the bathroom door snick closed and she squeezed her eyes shut, wondering what he would do if she sneaked into the bed before he came back; knowing it was futile because he would straightaway head for the sofa.

He didn't need her any more. Or he didn't want her. What did it matter which or both it was? They both hurt like hell. They both hurt like someone had ripped out her heart and torn it to shreds and trampled on the pieces.

Could injured pride feel this bad? Could

a miffed ego tear out your heart and rip it to shreds? Or had she been kidding herself and it had been Maureen who had been right all along?

Oh god, surely she hadn't fallen in love with Leo?

And yet all along she had known it was a risk, the greater risk; had known the possibility was there, the possibility to be drawn deeper and deeper under his spell until she could not bear the thought of being without him. All along she had known he had a heart of stone and still she had managed to do the unthinkable.

She'd fallen in love with him.

She lay there in the semi-gloom, the once silvery light of the moon now a dull grey, listening to him climb into bed, listening to him toss and turn and sigh, wishing him peace, even if he couldn't find it with her.

The scream woke him and he stilled with fear, hoping he'd imagined it. But then he heard the shouting, his father's voice, calling his mother those horrible names he didn't understand only to know they must be bad, and he cringed, waiting for the blow that would come at the end of his tirade. Then it came with a thump and his mother made a sound like a football when you kick it on the street and he vomited right there in his bed. He climbed out, weak and shaky, to the sound of his mother's cries, the bitter taste of sick in his mouth.

'Stamata,' he cried weakly through his tears, knowing he would be in trouble for messing up his bed, knowing his mother would be angry with him, wanting her to be angry with him so that things might be normal again. *'Stamato to tora.'* Stop it now!

And he pulled the door open and ran out, to see his father's fist raised high over his mother lying prostrate on the floor.

'Stamato to!' he screamed, running across the room, lashing out at his father, young fists flying, and earning that raised fist across his jaw as his reward, but not giving up. He couldn't stop, he had to try to make him stop hurting his mother.

He struck out again lashing at his father, but it was his mother who cried out and it made no sense, nor the thump of a body hitting the floor and then a baby screamed somewhere, and he blinked into consciousness, shaking and wet with perspiration, and waking to his own personal nightmare.

She was lying on the floor, looking dazed, tears springing from her eyes and her hand over her mouth where he must have hit her. And Sam screaming from the next room.

And he wanted to help. He knew he should help. He should do something.

But the walls caved in around him, his muscles remained frozen. Because, oh god, he was back in his past. He was back in that mean kitchen, his father shouting, his mother screaming and a child that saw too much.

And he wanted to put his hands over his ears and block it all out.

Oh god.

What had he done?

What had he done?

CHAPTER TWELVE

SHE blnked up at him warily, testing her aching jaw. 'I have to get Sam,' she said, wondering why he just sat there like a statue, wondering if that wild look in his eyes signalled that he was still sleeping, still lost in whatever nightmare had possessed him.

'I hit you,' he said at last, his voice a mere rasp, his skin grey in the moonlight.

'You didn't mean to,' she said, climbing to her feet. 'You were asleep. You were tossing and—'

'I hurt you.'

He had, but right now she was more concerned with the hurt in his eyes. With the raw, savage pain she saw there. And with reassuring her son, whose cries were escalating. 'It was an accident. You didn't mean it.'

'I warned you!'

'I have to see to Sam. Excuse me.' She rushed

around the bed to the dressing room and her distraught child, his tear streaked face giving licence for her own tears to fall. 'Oh Sam,' she whispered, kissing his tear stained cheek, pushing back the damp hair from his brow and clutching him tightly to her as she rocked him against her body. 'It's all right, baby,' she soothed, trying to believe it. 'It's going to be all right.'

She heard movement outside, things bumping and drawers being opened, but she dared not look, not until she felt her son's body relax against her, his whimpers slowly steadying. She waited a while, just to be sure, and then she kissed his brow and laid him back down in his cot.

And then she stood there a while longer, looking down at her child, his cheek softly illuminated in the moonlight, while she wondered what to do.

What did you do when your heart was breaking for a man who didn't want family? Who didn't want your love?

What could you do?

* * *

'What are you doing?' she asked when she emerged, watching Leo stashing clothes in a bag.

'I can't do this. I can't do this to you.'

'You can't do what to me?'

'I don't want to hurt you.'

'Leo, you were in the midst of a nightmare. I got too close. You didn't know I was there.'

He pulled open another drawer, extracted its contents. 'No. I know who I am. I know what I am. Pack your things, we're leaving.'

'No. I'm not going anywhere. Not before you tell me what's going on.'

'I can't do this,' he said in his frenzied state, 'to you and Sam.'

She sat on the bed and put a hand to her fore-head, stunned, while he opened another drawer, threw out more clothes. 'You're not making any sense.'

'It makes perfect sense!'

'No! It makes no sense at all! Why are you doing this? Because of a nightmare, because you accidentally lashed out and struck me?'

He walked stiffly up the bed, his chest heaving. 'Don't you understand, Evelyn, or Eve, or whoever you are, if I can do that to you asleep, how much more damage can I do when I am awake?'

And despite the cold chill in his words, she stood up and faced him, because she knew him well enough by now to know he was wrong. 'You wouldn't hit me.'

'You don't know that!' he cried, 'Nobody can know that,' giving her yet another hint of the anguish assailing him.

And Eve knew what she had to say; knew what she had to do; knew that she had to be brave. She moved closer, slowly, stopping before she reached him, but wanting to be close enough that he could see the truth of her words reflected on her face in the moonlight, close enough that she could pick up his hand and hold it to her chest so that he might feel her heart telling him the same message.

'I know it, because I've been with you Leo. I've spent nights filled with passion in your bed. I've spent days when you made me feel more alive than I have in my entire life. And I've seen the way you pulled my child from the sea when you saw him fall into the surf before I did. I know you would never harm him.'

She shook her head, amazed that she was about to confess something so very, very new; so very, very precious and tender, before she had even time to pull it out and examine it for all its flaws and weaknesses in private herself.

'Don't you see? I know it, Leo, because—' She sucked in air, praying for strength in order to confess her foolishness. Because hadn't he warned her not to get involved? Hadn't he told her enough times nothing could come of their liaison? But how else could she reach him? How else could she make him understand? 'Damn it, I know it because I love you.'

He looked down at her, his bleak eyes filled with some kind of terror before he shut them down, and she wondered what kind of hell she would see when he opened them again.

'Don't say that. You mustn't say that.' His words squeezed through his teeth, a cold, hard stiletto of pain that tore at her psyche, ripping into the fabric of her soul. But while it terrified her, at the same time she felt empowered. After all, what did she have left to lose? She'd already admitted the worst, she'd already laid her cards on the table. There was nothing left but to fight for this fledgling love, to defend it, and to defend her right to it.

'Why can't I say it, when it's the truth? And I know it's futile and pointless but it's there. I love you, Leo. Get used to it.'

'No! Saying I love you doesn't make everything all right. Saying I love you doesn't make it okay to beat someone.'

But he hadn't—

And suddenly a rush of cold drenching fear flooded down her spine along with the realisation that he wasn't talking about what had just taken place in this room. And whatever he had witnessed, it was violent and brutal and had scarred him deeply. 'What happened to you to make you believe yourself capable of these things? What horrors were you subjected to that won't let you rest at night?'

'The nightmares are a warning,' he said. 'A warning not to let this happen, and I won't. Not if it means hurting you and Sam.'

'But Leo—'

'Pack your things,' he said simply, sounding defeated. 'I'm taking you home.'

Melbourne was doing what it knew best, she thought as they touched down, offering up a bit of everything, the runway still damp from the latest shower, a bit of wind to tinker with the wings and liven up the landing and the sun peeping out behind a gilt edged cloud.

But it was so good to be home.

He insisted on driving her—or rather, having his driver drive them—and she wondered why he bothered coming along if he was going to be so glum and morose, unless it was so he could be sure she was gone.

And then they were there. At her house she had until now affectionately referred to as the hovel and never would again, because it was a home, a real home and it was hers and Sam's and filled with love and she was proud of it.

'Let me help you out,' Leo said and she wanted to tell him there was no need, that the driver would help unload and that she could manage, but there were bags and bags and a child seat and a sleeping Sam to carry inside, and it would have been churlish to refuse, and so she let him help.

Except what was she supposed to do with a billionaire in her house?

She had Sam on her hip, heavy with sleep, head lolling and clearly needing his cot while Leo deposited the last of her bags and her car seat, looking around him, looking like the world had suddenly been shrink wrapped and was too small for him. What on earth would he think of her tiny house and eclectic furniture after his posh hotels and private jet?

'Thank you,' she said, her heart heavy, not wanting to say goodbye but not wanting to delay the inevitable as clearly he looked for an exit. 'For everything.'

'It wouldn't work,' he offered, with a thumb to the place he knew he'd hurt her. 'It couldn't.'

She leaned into his touch, trying to hold it for as long as she possibly could, trying to imprint this very last touch on her memory. 'You don't know that,' she said. 'And now you'll never know.'

'There are things—' he started, before shaking

his head, his eyes sad. 'It doesn't matter. I know there is no way…'

'You know nothing,' she said, pulling away, stronger now for simply being home, by being back in her own environment, with her own bookshelves and ancient sofa and even her own faded rugs. 'But I do. I know how you'll end up if you walk out that door, if you turn your back on me and my love.

'You'll be like that old man in the picture in your suite, the old man sitting hunched and all alone on the park bench, staring out over the river and wondering whether he should have taken a chance, whether he should have taken that risk rather than playing it safe, rather than ending up all alone.

'You will be that man, Leo.'

He looked at her, his eyes bleak, his jaw set. He lifted a hand, put it one last time to Sam's head.

'Goodbye, Evelyn.'

CHAPTER THIRTEEN

EARLY summer wasn't one whole lot more reliable than spring, Eve reflected, as she looked up at the patchy blue sky, determined to risk the clothes line rather than using the dryer. Any savings on the electricity bill would be welcome. She'd picked up a couple of new clients recently, but things were still tight if she didnt want to dip into her savings.

Although of course, there was always the ring…

She'd taken it off in the plane, meaning to give it back to Leo but she'd forgotten in those gut wrenching final moments and he'd always said it was hers. Every day since then she checked her emails to see if he'd sent her some small message. Every time she found a recorded message, she punched the play button hoping, always hoping.

And after two weeks when he'd made no contact, out of spite or frustration or grief, she'd taken the ring to a jewellery shop to have it valued, staggered when she found out how much it was worth.

She wouldn't have to scrimp if she sold it.

But that had been nearly a month back and she hadn't been able to bring herself to do it.

Six weeks, she thought, as she pegged the first of her sheets to the line. Six weeks since that night in his suite, since that weekend in paradise. No wonder it seemed like a dream.

'Nice day,' called Mrs Willis, from over the fence. 'Reckon it'll rain later though.'

She glanced up at the sky, scowling at an approaching bank of cloud. 'Probably. How's Jack lately?'

'Going okay since they changed his meds. Sister reckons he's on the improve.' Her neighbour looked around. 'Where's Sam?'

'Just gone down for a nap,' Eve said, pegging up another sheet. 'Should be good for a couple of hours work.'

'Oh,' the older woman said. 'Speaking of work,

there's someone out the front to see you. Some posh looking bloke in a suit. Fancy car. Says he tried your door, but no answer. I told him I thought you were home though. I told him—'

Something like a lightning bolt surged down her spine. 'What did you say?' But she was already on her way, the sheets snapping in the breeze behind her. She touched a hand to the hair she'd tied back in a rough ponytail, then told herself off for even thinking it. Why did she immediately think it could be him? For all she knew it could be a courier delivery from one of her clients, although since when did courier drivers dress in posh suits and drive flash cars? Her heart tripping at a million miles an hour, nerves flapping and snapping like the sheets on the line, she allowed herself one deep breath, and then she opened the door.

There he stood. Gloriously, absolutely Leo, right there on her doorstep. He looked just as breathtakingly beautiful, his shoulders as broad, his hair so rich and dark and his eyes, his dark eyes looked different, there was sorrow there and pain, and something else swirling in the mix—hope?

And her heart felt it must be ten times its normal size the way it was clamouring around in there. But she'd had hopes before, had thought she'd seen cracks develop in his stone heart, and those hopes had been dashed.

'Leo,' she said breathlessly.

'Eve. You look good.'

She didn't look good. She had circles under her eyes, her hair was a mess and Mrs Willis had been on at her about losing too much weight. 'You look better.' And she winced, because it sounded so lame.

He looked around her legs. 'Where's Sam?'

'Nap time,' she said, and he nodded.

'Can I come in?'

'Oh.' She stood back, let him in. 'Of course.'

He looked just as awkward in her living room. 'I'll make coffee,' she suggested when he grabbed her hand, sending an electrical charge up her arm.

'No. I have to explain something first, Eve, if

you will listen. I need you to listen, to understand.'

She nodded, afraid to speak.

He took a deep breath once they were sitting on the sofa, his elbows using his knees for props as he held out his hands. 'I was not happy when I left you. I went to London, threw myself into the contract negotiations there; then to Rome and New York, and nowhere, nowhere could I forget you, nothing I could do, nothing I could achieve could blot out the thoughts of you.

'But I could not come back. I knew it could not work. But there was something I could do.'

She held her breath, her body tingling. Hoping.

'I hadn't seen my parents since I was twelve. I had to find them. It took— It took a little while to track them down, and then it was to discover my father was dead.'

She put a hand to his and he shook his head. 'Don't feel sorry. He was a sailor and a brutal, violent man. Everytime he was on leave he used my mother as a punching bag, calling her all sorts of vicious names, beating her senseless. I used to cower in fear behind my door, praying for it to stop. I was glad he was dead.'

He dragged in air. 'And the worst part of it—the worst of it was that he was always so full of remorse afterwards. Always telling her he was sorry, and that he loved her, even as she lay bruised and bleeding on the floor.'

Eve felt something crawl down her spine. A man who couldn't let himself love. A man who equated love with a beating. No wonder he felt broken inside. No wonder he was so afraid. 'Your poor mother,' she said, thinking, poor you.

He made a sound like a laugh, but utterly tragic. 'Poor mother. I thought so too. Until I was big enough to grow fists and hurt him like he hurt my mother. And my mother went to him. After everything he had done to her, she screamed at me and she went to him to nurse his wounds.' He dropped his head down, wrapped his arms over his head and breathed deep, shaking his head as he rose. 'She would not leave him, even when I begged and pleaded with her. She would not go. So I did. I slept at school. Friends gave me food. I got a job emptying rubbish bins. I begged on the streets. And it was the happiest I'd ever been.'

'Oh, Leo,' she said, thinking of the homeless child, no home to go to, no family…

'I left school a year later, went to work on the boats around the harbour. But I would not be a sailor like him, at that stage I didn't want to be Greek like him. So I learned from the people around me, speaking their languages, and started handling deals for people.

'I was good at it. I could finally make something of myself. But even though I could escape my world, I could not escape my past. I could not escape who I was. The shadow of my father was too big. The knowledge of what I would become…' His voice trailed off. 'I swore I would never let that happen to me. I would never love.'

She slipped a hand into one of his, felt his pain and his sorrow and his grieving. 'I'm so sorry it had to be that way for you. You should have had better.'

'Sam is blessed,' he said, shaking his head. 'Sam has a mother who fights for him like a tigress. His mother is warm and strong and filled with sunshine.' He lifted her hand, pressed it to his lips. 'Not like…'

And his words warmed her heart, even when she knew there was more he had to tell her. 'Did you find her then? Did you find your mother?'

His eyes were empty black, his focus nowhere, but someplace deep inside himself. 'She's in a home for battered women, broken and ill. She sits in a wheelchair all day looking out over a garden. She has nothing now, no-one. And as I looked at her, I remembered the words you said, about an old man sitting on a parkbench, staring at nothing, wishing he'd taking a chance…'

'Leo, I should never have said that. I had no right. I was hurting.'

'But you were right. When I looked at her, I saw my future, and for the first time, I was afraid. I didn't want it. Instead I wanted to take that chance that you offered me, like she should have taken that chance with me and escaped. But my father's shadow still loomed over me. My greatest fear was turning into him. Hurting you or Sam. I could not bear that.'

'You're not like that,' she said, tears squeezing from her eyes. 'You would never do that.'

'I couldn't trust myself to believe it. Until I was about to leave my mother's side and she told me the truth in her cracked and bitter voice, the truth that would have set me free so many years ago, but I never questioned what I had grown up believing. The truth that my father had come home after six months at sea and found her four months pregnant.'

'Leo!'

His eyes were bright and that tiny kernel of hope she'd seen there while he'd stood on her doorstep had flickered and flared into something much more powerful. 'He was impotent and she wanted a child and I was never his, Eve. I don't have to be that way. I don't have to turn into him.'

Tears blurred her vision, tears for the lost childhood, tears for the betrayal of trust between the parents and the child, the absence of a love that should have been his birthright. 'You would never have turned into him. I know.'

And he brought her hands to his lips and kissed them. 'You do things to me, Eve. You turn me inside out and upside down and I want to be with you, but I just don't know if I can do this. I don't know if I can love the way I should. The way you deserve.'

'Of course you can. It's been there, all along. You knew what was happening was wrong. You tried to save your mother. You tried to save me and Sam by cutting us loose. Because you didn't want to hurt us. You would never have done that if you hadn't cared, if you hadn't loved us, just a little.'

'I think…' He gave her a look that spoke of his confusion and fears. 'I think it's more than a little. These last weeks have been hell. I never want to be apart from you again. I want to wake up every morning and see your face next to mine. I want to take care of you and Sam, if you'll let me.'

She blinked across at him, unable to believe what she was hearing, but so desperately wanting it to be true. 'What are you saying?'

'I can't live without you. I need you.' He squeezed her hands, just as he squeezed the unfamiliar words from his lips. 'I love you.'

And she flew into his arms, big, fat tears of

happiness welling in her eyes. 'Oh Leo, I love you so much.'

'Oh my god, that's such a relief,' he said, clutching her tightly. 'I was afraid you would hate me for how I treated you.' He tugged her back, so he could look at her, brushing the hair from her face where it had got mussed. 'Because there's something else I need to know. Eve, will you take a chance on me. Would you consider becoming my wife?'

And her tears became a flood and she didn't care that she was blubbering, didn't care that she was a mess, only that Leo had loved her and wanted to marry her and life just couldn't get any better than that. 'Yes,' she said, her smile feeling like it was a mile wide, 'Yes, of course I will marry you.'

He pulled her into his kiss, a whirlpool of a kiss that spun her senses and sent her spirits and soul soaring.

'Thank you for coming into my life,' he said, drawing back, breathing hard. 'You are magical, Eve. You have brought happiness and hope to a place where there was only misery and darkness. How can I ever repay you?'

And she smiled up at his beautiful face, knowing he would never again live without love, not if she had anything to do with it. 'You can start by kissing me again.'

EPILOGUE

LEO Zamos loved it when a plan came together. He relished the cut and thrust of business, the negotiations, the sometimes compromise, the closing of the deal.

He lived for the adrenaline rush of the chase, and he lived for the buzz of success.

Or at least he had, until now.

These days he had other priorities.

He shook Culshaw's hand, who was still beaming with the honour of walking Eve down the aisle before leaving him chatting to Mrs Willis about the weather. He looked around and found his new bride standing in the raised gazebo where they'd been married a little while ago. She was holding Sam's hand as Hannah jigged him on her hip, the sapphire ring sparkling on her finger nestled alongside a new matching plain band.

Evelyn—Eve—he still couldn't decide which he liked best, had always looked more like a goddess than any mere mortal, but today, in her slim fitting lace gown, her hair piled high and curling in tendrils around her face and pinned with a long gossamer thin veil that danced in the warm tropical breeze, she was the queen of goddesses, and she was his. She laughed as her veil was caught in the breeze, the ends tickling Sam's face and making him squeal with delight. And then, as if aware he was watching, as if feeling the tug of his own hungry gaze, she turned her head, turned those brilliant blue eyes on him, her laughter faltering as their eyes connected on so many different levels before her luscious mouth turned up into a wide smile.

And it was physically impossible for his feet not to take the quickest and most direct route through the guests until he was at her side, his arm snaked around her waist pulling her in tight, taking Sam's free hand with the other.

'How is my beautiful new family enjoying today?'

And Sam pulled both hands free and pointed, 'Boat!'

'Sam is beside himself,' Eve said, as Hannah put him down and let him run to the other side of the gazebo to gaze out between the slats at the sailing boat lazily cruising past the bay.

'Culshaw's the same. Asking him to give you away has made his year, I'd say.'

'I like him,' she said, as they watched him animatedly tell Mrs Willis a story. 'He feels like family to me.'

'Canny old devil,' he said as he folded his arms around her. 'Did I tell you what he said when I tried to apologise and tell him that we hadn't really been engaged that weekend in Melbourne? He actually said, "poppycock, everyone knew you were destined to be together",' and Eve laughed.

'Maureen told me the same thing.'

'And they were right,' he said, drawing her back into the circle of his arms, kissing her lightly on the head. 'You are my destiny, Eve, my beautiful wife.'

'Oh,' she said, turning in the circle of his arms. 'Did you hear the Alvarezes' news?'

He frowned, 'I'm not sure I did.'

'Felicity is pregnant. They're both thrilled. I couldn't be happier.'

He nodded. 'That is good news, but at the risk of trying to make you happier, I have a small present for you.'

'But you've already given me so much.'

'This is special. Culshaw's agreed to sell Mina Island. It's yours now, Evelyn.'

'What?' Her eyes shone bright with incredulity. 'It's mine? Really?'

'Yours and Sam's. Everything of mine is now yours, but this is especially for you both. It's a wedding gift and a thank you gift and an I love you gift all rolled into one. And it guarantees you can bring Sam back when he's older any time you want and show him everything he missed out on now.'

'Oh, Leo,' she said, her eyes bright with tears, 'I don't know what to say. It's too much. I have nothing for you.'

He shook his head. 'It's nowhere near enough.

It was here that you gave me the greatest gift of all. You gave me back my heart. You taught me how to love. How can I ever repay you for that?'

She cupped his cheek against her palm, her cereulean eyes filled with love, and he took that hand and pressed his lips upon it. 'I love you, Evelyn Zamos.'

'Oh, Leo, I love you so very, very much.'

They were the words he needed to hear, the words that set his newly unlocked heart soaring. He kissed her then, in the white gazebo covered with sweetly scented flowers, kissed her in the perfumed air as the breeze set the palm tree fronds to rustling and the sail boat gracefully cruised by.

'Boat!' yelled Sam to the sound of wobbly footsteps, suddenly tugging at their legs, pointing out to sea. 'Boat!'

And laughing, Leo scooped the boy up in his arms and they all gazed out over the sapphire blue water to watch the passing vessel. 'How long, do you think,' he whispered to the woman at his side, 'is the perfect age gap between children?'

She looked up at him on a blink. 'I don't know. Some people say two to three years.'

'In that case,' he said, with a chaste kiss to her forehead and a very unchaste look in his eyes, 'I have a plan.'

* * * * *

Mills & Boon® Large Print
December 2011

BRIDE FOR REAL
Lynne Graham

FROM DIRT TO DIAMONDS
Julia James

THE THORN IN HIS SIDE
Kim Lawrence

FIANCÉE FOR ONE NIGHT
Trish Morey

AUSTRALIA'S MAVERICK MILLIONAIRE
Margaret Way

RESCUED BY THE BROODING TYCOON
Lucy Gordon

SWEPT OFF HER STILETTOS
Fiona Harper

MR RIGHT THERE ALL ALONG
Jackie Braun

Mills & Boon® Large Print

January 2012

THE KANELLIS SCANDAL
Michelle Reid

MONARCH OF THE SANDS
Sharon Kendrick

ONE NIGHT IN THE ORIENT
Robyn Donald

HIS POOR LITTLE RICH GIRL
Melanie Milburne

FROM DAREDEVIL TO DEVOTED DADDY
Barbara McMahon

LITTLE COWGIRL NEEDS A MUM
Patricia Thayer

TO WED A RANCHER
Myrna Mackenzie

THE SECRET PRINCESS
Jessica Hart

1211 Rom LP